WHITE RIVER WOLVES

SABLE'S FIRE

DAWN SULLIVAN

All rights reserved. No part of this publication may be reproduced, stored in a retrieval system, or transmitted in any form or by means mechanical, electronic, photocopying, recording or otherwise without prior permission from the author. This is a work of fiction. Names, characters, places and events are fictitious in every regard. Any similarities to actual events or persons, living or dead are purely coincidental. Any trademarks, service marks, product names or featured names are assumed to be the property of their respective owners and are used only for reference. There is no implied endorsement of any of these terms are used. Except for review purposes, the reproduction of this book in whole or in part, mechanically or electronically, constitutes a copyright violation. Published in the United States of America in June 2018; Copyright 2018 by Dawn Sullivan. The right of the Author's Name to be identified as the Author of the Work has been asserted by them in accordance with The Copyright, Designs and Patent Act of 1988.

Published by Dawn Sullivan

Cover Design: Dana Leah with Designs by Dana

Photographer: Robin's Clicks

Model: Kathryn Ann

Copyright 2018 © Author Dawn Sullivan

Language: English

For Polly. Thank you for all of your continued support, and for introducing me to your daughter, who is the perfect Sable.

1

"Come on, Sable. This will be fun," Aiden teased, slipping an arm around her shoulders and pulling her close, his voice full of laughter. "It will be just like the old days."

Raising an eyebrow, she pulled slightly away from him as she asked, "You mean like last week, when you took me to a bar, and then expected me to find my own way home while you left with a hot piece of ass you found to warm your bed that night?" She was still pissed at him for it. At least the bastard left her his truck so she didn't have to call a cab.

"Damn, Aiden," River's voice slipped into the ear coms they wore, "you sure know how to treat a lady."

Aiden chuckled softly as he opened the door to the Blue Moon Bar, letting his arm slide down so his hand rested on the small of her back. "I was just helping the little kitty to her car. But, when we got there, I realized she was too drunk to drive."

"So, you had to take her home," Sable said dryly,

moving away from him when he tried to slip his arm around her waist. "Tell me, Aiden, how was she supposedly so drunk when she is a shifter? She would have had to drink a shit ton of alcohol, and all I remember seeing her sip on was one glass of wine, that she didn't even finish."

"Wait. Let's go back to the kitty part," Trigger interrupted, his tone low and interested. "I like kitties. Especially ones with a wild side."

Sable barely resisted the urge to slam her fist in Aiden's gut when he replied, "This kitty definitely had claws, Trigger. You would have loved her."

"Do you have eyes on the target?"

Sable stiffened when her alpha's voice broke through their light bantering, and her gaze slowly scanned the interior of the packed bar. "Negative, boss."

"It's still early," River muttered. "Cinderella isn't supposed to be here for another thirty minutes."

Rolling her eyes at the target's code name, Sable pasted a smile on her face and slowly walked around the room, finally allowing Aiden to slip an arm around her waist, even though she didn't want to.

"That's if the information we got is correct, or if she even decides to make an appearance," Trigger grunted, his breathing slow and easy through the coms. He was good at his job, as was the rest of the team, but Trigger seemed to have more patience than most. Sable thought that was probably from the years he spent in the military, years that he never talked about. He kept his secrets from the past to himself, and hid behind an arrogant exterior. He was a pain in the ass, but was also one of the first people she would want on her side in a fight. Yes, he had secrets, but so did she. She wasn't going to hold that against the man.

"She'll show," Aiden said confidently, sending Sable a cocky grin.

"How do you know?" Charlotte asked.

"Because, she will be too afraid not to. When her fiancé tells someone to do something, they do it. He doesn't tell them twice." Sable nodded, knowing it was the truth. They'd gotten word earlier in the day that he'd told Cinderella to be at the Blue Moon Bar by 7 p.m., even going into detail regarding what she was to wear. There was no doubt in Sable's mind that their target would be there, and she would probably be early just to avoid pissing the bastard off.

"I will never let a man control me like that," Charlotte vowed darkly.

"Me neither," Sable agreed. "I'll cut his balls off and feed them to him first."

Aiden cringed, glancing down at her. "That's a little bloodthirsty, don't you think?"

"Just don't piss me off," she said, crossing the room to a table by the far wall, and sliding up into the high bar stool next to it. Leaning back against the wall, she scanned the room again, unaware that she was tapping the table with her fingernails in agitation.

Sable flinched when Aiden took the seat across from her, and reached across the table to cover her hand with his. Clenching her teeth together, she forced herself to keep her hand where it was, even though everything in her told her to snatch it away fast.

She was being stupid, and she knew it, but the way Aiden had been treating her lately just plain sucked. He was her best friend, the one she went with to almost everything, but his attitude toward her had changed in the past few weeks. Ever since his brother found his mate, it felt like Aiden was pushing her away for some reason. He started spending less time with her, and more time either at the gym, taking on extra shifts for Chase to ensure their compound was safe, or at the bar in town. Before Xavier and Janie got together, Aiden never went to the bar without her. Now, he was there at least a couple times a week, and she sometimes wondered if he went looking for a mate of his own. She hated to admit it, but it fucking hurt.

"So, tell me more about this kitty, Aiden," Trigger demanded, and Sable had to bite her tongue before she said something she might regret.

"Hey," Aiden said quietly, squeezing her hand as he leaned over the table closer to her. "What's wrong?"

Aware that everyone could hear their conversation, Sable tugged her hand from his and looked away. Sliding her fingers roughly through her dark hair, she barely held back a snarl as she replied, "Nothing. Just trying to do my job."

She saw the confusion in Aiden's eyes, and knew he scented her lie when he whispered, "Sable? Talk to me."

Refusing to get into it with him while they were on a mission, Sable shook her head, glancing around the room. When she did, she caught a glimpse of a tall, curvy woman with long, blonde hair walking across the floor toward a hallway with a sign that said restrooms above the doorway. She knew instantly it was the target they were sent to save after all of the pictures she'd studied of her.

"I see Cinderella, Alpha," Sable said, sliding out of her

chair and making her way to the other side of the room, leaving Aiden behind. "She's going to the bathroom."

"Follow her."

"Already on it."

"A black sedan just pulled up in front of the bar," Charlotte said calmly. "Two men are getting out, and they are huge. One has a crew cut and tats down both arms. The other is dressed to kill, in a suit."

"It's her fiancé," Chase muttered.

"They are both packing heat, boss, and a lot of it."

Chase swore darkly, before growling, "Aiden and Sable, get her and get the hell out of there."

"I'm pulling around back," Xavier told them. "Hurry up."

Ignoring the curse Aiden bit out behind her, Sable ran down the hall, grabbing the surprised woman's arm before she could slip into the bathroom. "I don't have time to explain who I am right now, Grace, but you need to come with me. And we need to go now!"

Biting her lip, the woman looked down at where Sable held her and whispered, "I'm sorry? You must have the wrong person."

Sable could smell the fear wafting off Grace, along with the stench of her lie. "I know you are scared, but we may not get another opportunity like this. Grace, please, your fiancé is coming into the bar as we speak. We are here to help you, but you have to come with us now. There isn't much time."

Her eyes widening in terror, Grace whispered, "He's here already?"

"Yes," Sable said, urging her down the hall toward the back exit.

Grace came to a stop, shaking her head. "I can't go with you. If Jared finds out, he will hunt you down and kill you. I can't let that happen."

"You don't worry about us, Ma'am," Aiden said, looking back toward the bar. "This isn't our first rodeo."

"No, but if you don't get moving, it could be your last," River hissed through the coms.

"They are on their way into the bar," Charlotte warned softly. "If I have to take them out, I need to do it now."

"Not necessary," Sable said, pushing open the back door, and shoving Grace through it. "We're clear."

A black SUV sat at the end of the alley, and taking Grace by the elbow, Sable quickly guided her to it, opening the door. "Get in." Not waiting for a response, she nudged the woman inside, jumping in behind her. Once Aiden rounded the vehicle and got in on the other side, Xavier stepped on the gas pedal and they took off.

"All clear," Charlotte said quietly. "We will meet you back at the plane."

"Who are you?" Grace whispered, her gaze going from Sable to Aiden, and then to the men in the front of the vehicle.

Chase looked back at her and gave her a small smile. "Your saviors, Miss Carmichael. We were contacted by the council and asked to remove you from an abusive situation."

"The Council?" she whispered, her eyes growing wide. "How did they know?" Her brow furrowing, she answered her own question before he could. "My brother."

"He did it out of love," Sable said softly, patting Grace's hand lightly with her own. "So that you could have the chance at a life he never got."

Her eyes glittering with tears, Grace begged, "Can you save him, too? I know he got tied up in Jared's business, but Mathew really is a good man."

Sable shook her head sadly, hating the reply she had to give her. "I'm sorry, Grace, but when the council sent someone to his home to extract him, they were too late. Someone must have found out that he contacted them."

"No!" Grace rasped, her eyes filling with tears that escaped, falling down her cheeks. "Please, no!"

Sable slipped an arm around Grace's shoulders, pulling her close, wishing there was something she could say or do to make her feel better. "I'm so sorry," she whispered, knowing they were just empty words. "We are taking you to the council now, and they will place you somewhere safe. Somewhere you will be happy."

"How can I be happy if I'm alone?" Grace whispered, grasping Sable's hand tightly.

Sable kept quiet, knowing there was nothing she could say that would help soothe the woman now. She'd just lost her brother, the only family she had, along with her life as she knew it. All because of a dark, dangerous bear shifter who ran the large city she lived in, who demanded she mate with him even though they were not fated mates.

Glancing over at Aiden, Sable sighed. Fate was a fickle bitch, deciding who belonged to whom. As much as she wanted Aiden to be hers, she knew he wasn't, and she needed to come to terms with that. He was her best friend, and a part of her would always love him, but he would never be hers.

2

Daxton Dreher pulled up in front of the large cottage-style home, sighing as he put his truck into park and leaned his head back against the seat. He was finally home. He'd been gone for ten years, with little to no communication with his family, and he missed them terribly. Serving as a warrior for his king was one of the most exciting things he had ever done in his forty-five years of life, but he was glad it was over.

Swinging open his door, Dax slid out of the vehicle and raised his arms to stretch. He'd driven over fifteen hours straight just so that he could get home today. It was his little sisters' birthday, and he couldn't wait to see the surprise in their eyes when they saw him. He had always been close with both Raven and Rubi. They were eighteen years younger than him, and had followed him everywhere as children, and he let them. He took them to the movies with him, the library, and even to his warrior training sessions with his friends. He was the one who taught them both how to shift when they struggled with it at a young age, and also taught them the importance of not doing it in front of humans. The three of them were inseparable, until he left to serve the king. He would have stayed home if he could have, but he wasn't given a choice. When the king of the dragons demanded your presence, you went. No questions asked. All dragon warriors were required to serve under royalty for a five year period. When it was requested of Dax, he stayed on another five years. Thank fuck a third request never came. He would have had to figure out how to tell his king no, which was never recommended.

When the front door of the house slammed open, and his sister, Rubi, stormed out dressed in tight, black leather pants, a dark red shirt covered in a black leather jacket, and sporting a Glock at her waist and knives in her boots, he raised his eyes and drawled, "Hey, sprite, what kind of war are we fighting today?"

Rubi froze, and then squeaked his name before closing the distance between them and launching herself into his arms. "Dax, oh God, I'm so glad you're home! I wanted to call you so many times, but they wouldn't let me. They refused to tell me how to get a hold of you."

She had to be talking about his parents. They were the only ones who were given a way to contact him when he left. The king thought it was best if his warriors had little to no communication with family while working for him. He wanted their focus on the well-being of him and his family, not their own. Frowning in confusion, Dax slowly pushed her back from him, clasping her arms gently as he asked, "Rubi, talk to me, sweetheart. What's wrong?"

She raised her head, looking up at him with bright

amber eyes full of pain and sorrow. "She's gone, Dax. And no matter how hard I try, I can't find her anywhere."

"Who's gone?"

"Raven," his mother said roughly from the doorway. "She was taken from us over a year ago, Dax. Stolen in the middle of the night."

His eyes flew from Rubi to his mother, anger rising in him as he growled, "Who took her, Mother?"

"We don't know," Rubi whispered, tears streaming down her face. "But, I have my suspicions."

"Rubi, no!"

Yanking her arms from Dax, Rubi turned to glower at their mother, resting her hands on her hips as she snarled, "I refuse to keep quiet any longer, Mother! You and Dad can hide in that damn house, praying Raven somehow miraculously returns, but I'm done! She's my sister! Can you imagine what she is going through, wherever she is? She probably thinks we have abandoned her." Turning, snapping dark amber eyes his way, she growled, "I'm finding her, Dax. Are you in?"

"Raven is gone, Rubi," his father said, appearing behind his mother. "You need to let this go. You are only making your mom suffer more."

"Bullshit," Rubi snapped.

"Wait," Dax said, holding up a hand for silence. Looking between his parents and Rubi, he asked, "I don't understand. Raven was kidnapped, but you don't want us to look for her? Why?"

"Because," Rubi growled, claws emerging from her fingers as she glared at their parents, "they were a part of it, Dax. They sold her to someone, I just can't figure out who."

"What the fuck," he snarled, his own claws lengthening and his fangs punching through his gums as he slowly began to stalk toward his mother and father, stopping just in front of them. "What is she talking about?"

"Who the hell knows?" his father snarled. "She's delusional, son. Has been since Raven was taken."

Dax scented the acrid smell of his father's lies, and ignoring his mother's whispered pleas, he wrapped his hand around the bastard's throat and slammed him up against the side of the house. "You *sold* my sister?"

"Dax, we didn't have a choice," his mother cried.

Dax turned his fury on his mother, his lips pealing back from his teeth as he snarled, "There is always a choice, Mother. You made the wrong one."

"Philip Perez is not someone you deny, Dax," his father said, his own fangs lengthening as he clawed at Dax's hand. "If you do, your entire family ends up dead."

"So, you were worried about your own miserable life, but not the life of your child? How much did you get for her, Dad? Fifty thousand? A hundred?"

His eyes bulging, his dad sputtered, "Dax. Stop this. Now!"

"How much?" Dax ground out, his hand tightening around his father's throat.

"Twenty-five thousand, Dax," his mother cried, as she tugged on his arm, trying to pull him away from his father. "It was twenty-five thousand. We were to take it, and never talk about what happened to anyone."

"Hush money," Rubi said from behind him. "So, I was right."

"You bastards." How could they have sold his little sister like that? Shaking his head, Dax slowly squeezed harder, before finally letting up and tossing his father across the porch as if he were nothing. "You aren't worth it. Rubi, grab a bag. We're getting out of here." There was no way in hell he was leaving her behind.

"I don't live here," Rubi said, her voice hard with anger. "I haven't since I first began to suspect what they did. And, I always have a to-go bag in my car. I'm ready."

"But, where are you going?" his mother whispered, from where she now knelt by his dad. "You just got home."

Did she really think he was going to sit around and play the good son after everything they'd done? They sold his fucking sister! "Anywhere but here."

3

Sable stood in front of her alpha's door, knowing what she was about to do was the best thing for her right now, even if it was one of the hardest things she'd ever done. She loved her family, loved her pack, but she needed to get away. Needed time to think about things that she couldn't think about with Aiden so near. There really was no other choice. Taking a deep breath, she raised her hand and knocked.

"Come in."

Opening the door, Sable stepped inside, closing it quietly behind her. Chase sat at his desk, a welcoming smile on his face. His mate, Angel, stood behind him, a hand on his shoulder. It hurt her heart knowing that she was about to leave them. "Thank you for seeing me," she said softly, struggling with where to start.

Motioning to a chair in front of the desk, Angel smiled gently, "Have a seat, Sable. I know why you are here, and I think I have a solution."

Sable stiffened, averting her eyes to a point over the

alpha mate's shoulder. "I would appreciate it if you would stay out of my head, please," she said tightly, knowing she was being borderline insubordinate right now, but she couldn't help it. Her thoughts and feelings were hers and hers alone. The only way someone else should know what they were is if she decided to share them herself. Unfortunately, Angel had certain gifts that allowed her to see into people's minds, and it would seem she had taken advantage of those gifts now.

"I'm sorry," Angel apologized, walking around the desk to sit in a chair beside her. "Normally, I try not to intrude, but you have been broadcasting your thoughts loudly lately." When Sable gasped in dismay, Angel placed a hand on hers, squeezing it gently. "No one knows what Chase and I know, Sable. I haven't told anyone else. I promise, I would never violate your trust like that."

"Neither would I," Chase said gruffly, leaning forward to place his arms on the top of the desk. "However, I am glad that Angel came to me about it."

Sable dropped her gaze to stare at the floor, admitting softly, "I'm ashamed of myself and the way I feel."

"What?" Angel gasped, kneeling down beside her and cupping her cheek in the palm of her hand. "Never feel ashamed for loving someone, Sable. Love is everything."

"Not if it isn't returned, or can never be," Sable whispered, swiping at a tear that escaped.

"There is no doubt in my mind that Aiden loves you, too," Angel said softly.

"He loves me like a sister," Sable said, hating the way her voice wobbled. "Like a friend."

"There are many different ways to love someone."

Sable nodded, a breath hitching in her throat as she replied, "Yes, there are."

"I think, in time, you will see that what you feel for Aiden isn't the forever kind of love. Nor is it the love that you feel for a mate," Angel told her gently. "I've been around a long time, Sable, and I have only recently found out the difference of loving someone and being in love with them. When you meet your mate, you will see what I'm talking about."

"Aiden isn't my mate."

"No," Angel agreed, running a hand gently down Sable's hair, "he isn't. But, your mate is out there somewhere, waiting for you. Trust me, you wouldn't want to commit yourself to someone else, when you could have so much more with the one who completes the other half of your soul."

"She's right," Chase said quietly. "I was alone for a long time before Angel finally made an appearance. And, I wouldn't have it any other way."

Sable grasped Angel's hand tightly in hers, smiling through her tears. "Thank you, both. I hope, one of these days, I find the kind of love that you are talking about."

"You will," Angel murmured softly, before rising to her feet and walking back around the desk to once again stand beside her mate. "Now, about that possible solution I told you that I have."

"We have a mission for you, Sable," Chase said, handing her a manila envelope. Sable stiffened at the look in her alpha's clear blue eyes, one that spoke of the importance of the assignment they were about to give her.

"My team and I have been looking into possible leads regarding the abduction of Aiden and Xavier's sister,"

Angel told her, gesturing to the envelope. "Everything we have is in there. We believe she is somewhere on the east coast, and is possibly with coyote shifters."

"Coyote? Are you sure?" That could be bad. It was no secret that coyotes and wolves did not get along. She did not know of any instances where they could co-exist.

"Unfortunately, yes," Angel confirmed. "I want you to take two enforcers of your choice with you, and investigate all of the places on the list in that envelope. There are both wolf and coyote packs, but we are leaning toward the coyote ones for this. If you suspect she is with one of the packs, contact us."

"What about extraction?"

Angel glanced at Chase, deferring to him. "You have permission to extract only if necessary, and if you can do it safely without putting your team in jeopardy. If not, you call us. Angel will bring reinforcements."

"I will take Charlotte and…" Sable paused, unsure who to name next. Normally, it would be Aiden, but obviously that wasn't going to happen this time. Not only was the whole idea to get away from him for a while, but she was looking for his sister. She didn't want Aiden or Xavier involved unless she was actually able to track the missing girl down. There was no way she was taking Trigger. He was a pain in the ass, even if he was good at what he did. She could take River, but if she did, that wouldn't leave many enforcers for Chase if he received another mission for the council. There was only one choice. "Silver."

His eyes narrowing, Chase asked, "Are you sure? She hasn't been training with us for very long."

"No," Sable replied, "but she's good, and I trust her."

She didn't know what it was about Janie's sister, but she did trust her, and the wolf could kick some serious ass.

"Done," Chase decided. "Make sure to check in at least every other day so we know you are safe."

"Also, keep your eyes and ears open for the General, Sable," Angel cut in. "Last I heard, he was still recovering from his altercation with Chase, but don't ever underestimate his power or his reach."

"Altercation," Chase sneered. "I was so close to tearing that fucker's throat out. Next time, I'm going to do it. No one messes with my family."

Placing her hand on Chase's shoulder, Angel went on, "There is no reason to believe that the General is involved in any of this, but he has bases all over the United States, which includes a large one in Washington, D.C."

Sable nodded, knowing the General was a force to be reckoned with. She had no desire to go up against him without more backup with her than Charlotte and Silver. He had already kidnapped, tortured, and killed so many people. She didn't want to be added to the list. "We will watch out for his men."

"Good."

Sable rose, her gaze going from Chase to Angel. She knew this mission was one of the most important ones they could have given her, and the fact that they trusted her to be in charge of it filled her with pride. "I won't let you down," she promised.

"We know you won't," Angel said, a slow smile crossing her face.

As Sable left, she didn't see the look that her alphas exchanged. Nor did she hear Angel whisper, "Good luck, my friend."

4

An hour later, Sable sat at her kitchen table going over the contents of the envelope. There were a total of eight coyote packs on the list for them to look into, along with a couple of wolf packs. She shivered when she saw that two of them were in D.C. As strong as she appeared on the outside, the idea of being caught by the General and his men terrified her. After all of the hell he'd put her friends through, she wanted nothing more than to put a bullet in his heart, but she wasn't stupid. She knew what he did to his female prisoners, and she was going to stay as far away from him and his goons as possible without more than just Charlotte and Silver as backup, if she could help it.

Straightening in her chair, Sable set the list aside and started combing through the files in front of her. There was no place for her fear on this mission. She needed to shove it down ruthlessly, just like she always did. All that mattered was Aiden and Xavier's sister. Finding her and bringing her home to her brothers was the important thing.

There was a knock on her door, and then Charlotte and Silver walked in without waiting for her to get up and answer it. Going to her fridge, Charlotte pulled out a beer and tossed it to Silver, and then grabbed one for herself before taking a seat across from Sable.

"What's up, girl? Why did you call us here?"

"No alcohol," Sable said, grabbing the can from her friend before she could pop the tab.

"Well, shit, I was looking forward to that."

Sable heard Silver snicker behind her, before setting her beer on the counter and sliding into the chair beside her. "Who drinks before noon, anyway?"

Charlotte shrugged and grinned, "Hey, I'm not on duty today, and it's five o'clock somewhere!"

"Actually, as of right now, you are both on duty," Sable told them, tapping the stack of files in front of her. "We have a mission, and ladies, it's an important one. We can't afford to fuck it up."

Charlotte immediately became serious, wiping the smirk from her face. "Just the three of us?"

Sable nodded. "Chase and Angel are sending me east, and told me to take two enforcers with me."

"You chose me?" Silver asked in surprise. "But, you've never seen me in action before. How do you know I can be what you need me to be when we are out there?"

Sable grinned, "I see you in action on a daily basis, Silver. You may not have been on an actual mission with us before, but it is obvious that you will be a huge asset to our team."

Silver's dark grey eyes went from Sable to Charlotte,

and a slow smile spread across her lips. "Well, then, I'm in!"

Charlotte raised her hand and fist bumped Silver's, but then turned a questioning gaze to Sable. "I'm definitely in, too, but I don't understand why they are only sending us? They never do that. We go as a team, and Chase leads it."

"This assignment is sensitive," Sable told them, "and what I am about to say goes no further than the three of us." After they both nodded in agreement, she went on, "We are being sent to look for Aiden and Xavier's sister."

"Sister?" Charlotte asked in confusion. "I didn't know they had a sister."

"She was stolen from them years ago," Sable explained quietly. "When they were just boys, their father's obsession with power consumed him, and he made a deal with another pack, selling us out because he wanted to become the alpha of the White River Wolves. Titen let the other pack onto our lands so they could attack us, but in the end, they turned against him. He was able to hide Aiden and Xavier, but his wife was nine months pregnant at the time. They killed her, cut her open, and stole the baby. No one has been able to find her since."

"You have got to be fucking kidding me!" Silver snarled, smacking her hand down on the table. "Who in the hell does something like that?"

Charlotte's eyes misted with tears as she whispered, "That's horrible. How old would she be now, Sable?"

"Twenty," Sable said quietly.

"And we have no idea what she has been going through since those bastards kidnapped her?"

"No," Sable admitted, "which is one of the reasons this mission stays between us. Aiden and Xavier have been through enough. We have no idea what this girl will be like when we find her. Hell, we don't even know if we will be able to find her. It's best if we keep things quiet for now."

"Agreed," both women replied in unison.

"So, we have leads to check out?" Charlotte asked, reaching for one of the files.

"Angel and her team have compiled files on ten packs for us to look into on the east coast, eight coyote and two wolf."

"Coyote!" Silver gasped, her eyes widening in horror.

"My sentiments exactly," Sable bit out, sliding the list over in front of them. "We are going to start in Virginia, but I need to warn you. From what I have been told, we need to be very careful. One of the General's biggest bases is in the D.C. area."

"Fuck the General," Silver snarled, her eyes darkening in anger. "After what that son of a bitch did to my sister, I will gut the bastard if I see him."

"Hell, yeah," Charlotte growled, her eyes going wolf as her fangs dropped. "After everything he's done to our friends, that prick deserves to die."

Their words filled Sable with determination and courage, and she raised her hand, curling it into a fist and holding it out in front of her. "Fuck the General," she agreed, smiling in satisfaction when the others bumped their fists into hers.

It was late afternoon before they were finished going through the files and had a plan in place. Deciding it was best to leave immediately, they each went their separate ways to pack a bag and gear up. Forty-five minutes later, they were throwing their things into the trunk of Sable's black sports car, when she heard Aiden's voice.

"Where are you heading, Sable?"

Taking a deep breath, she slammed the trunk shut and motioned for Charlotte and Silver to get in the car. "We are going away for a bit." She had to watch what she said, because he would be able to scent a lie.

"Where?"

"They are looking into a few things for me, Aiden," a deep voice said. Sable glanced over to see Chase walking toward them with his niece, Lily, in his arms.

"Alone?" Aiden asked, his eyes narrowing as his gaze went from her, to Charlotte and Silver.

"What? You think we can't handle it alone?" Sable snapped back.

"I never said that," Aiden growled, reaching out to grab her arm. She yanked it away, and stepped back. "What the hell is wrong with you, Sable?"

"She's sad," Lily said quietly.

"What?"

"Sable's sad," the little girl repeated, walking over to put her hand gently on Sable's arm.

"What's she talking about, Sable?" Aiden demanded. "Why are you upset?"

Sable swallowed hard, raising her hand and running her fingers lightly down Lily's hair. "I'm just going through some things right now, Aiden. I'll be fine."

Lily gave her a blinding smile as she said, "Yes, you will be. You will be very happy soon."

"I will?" Sable murmured, praying the little girl was

right. She knew Lily had gifts, had even seen it for herself several times, but she'd never been on the receiving end of the child's premonitions.

Lily tugged on her arm until she knelt in front of the girl, and then she leaned in close. "When you meet him, don't be afraid," she whispered loudly.

"When I meet who?"

"The man who will make you smile again," Lily said, touching Sable's face softly. "He won't hurt you, and neither will his fire."

"His fire?"

Lily's nose scrunched up slightly, and she nodded slowly. "Yes, it's bright, and hot, but he will only use it to keep you safe."

"What in the hell is she talking about, Chase?" Aiden demanded loudly.

Before Sable could say anything, Chase growled, "You will treat my niece with respect, pup!"

"Yes, Alpha," Aiden bit out, baring his neck in deference to his alpha, even as his eyes glittered in anger.

Sable ignored him, her eyes never leaving Lily's as she covered the little girl's hand with hers. "I'm going to meet him soon?"

"Yes," Lily said softly. "He's looking for someone, just like you. But, she's lost for now."

Sable stared into eyes that were so much older and wiser than the seven-year-old child in front of her. She hesitated before asking, "Who is he looking for?"

"Someone he loves very much. The bad men took her, and he can't find her. He's sad, like you."

"Who...who is she to him, Lily? Do you know? Can you see?" Sable stumbled over the words, confused by the conversation. Who was this man who would make her smile again? Who was he looking for?

"She's his family," Lily said simply.

Unwilling to push her further, Sable pulled Lily close and gave her a tight hug. "Thank you, sweetheart. I will watch for him. I promise."

"And don't be afraid."

"I won't."

Sable rose, leaning down to give Lily one last hug before nodding to her alpha and Aiden, and then walking around the car to open the driver's side door. She paused when she heard Lily call her name. "Yes?"

"You need to hurry. Dax is about to be caught soon."

Sable's eyes widened in surprise, and she whispered, "Dax?"

Lily nodded solemnly. "They are going to hurt him."

5

Daxton stopped the truck in front of what was left of the mansion that used to be owned by Colombian drug lord Philip Perez, cursing loudly at the sight of piles of mass destruction. He knew the bastard was dead, but had held out hope that there would be something left behind to point them in the right direction. By the looks of it, there wasn't going to be anything left to find. It was all destroyed.

His hands tightening on the steering wheel, Dax growled lowly, fighting a losing battle with the beast inside him. It wanted to break free and tear through the rubble in front of him searching for his sister, even though he knew Raven was long gone.

Rubi swore softly as she opened her door and stepped out. "What are we going to do now, Dax?"

Lowering his head, he took a deep breath as a shudder racked his body, a deep groan emerging as tiny beads of sweat appeared all over his body. Shoving his dragon ruthlessly back down, he gritted his teeth tightly until he knew he was back in control.

"Dax?"

Slowly, raising his head, Dax looked over at his sister. She was once again dressed in leather, which seemed to be her choice of clothing now. The Glock was at her waist, and he could see the handle of a knife peeking out of each boot. What surprised him today, was the sword at her back. They trained weekly with swords when she was a child, but it was all for fun. Dragon warriors used them to defend the king, but normally, the women never trained and fought. He'd included his sisters in his lessons, approved by the trainer, because he wanted them to be able to take care of themselves when he was called upon to serve the king. He never thought they would ever really have to defend themselves with one.

Rubi cocked an eyebrow, her long, light blonde hair spilling over one shoulder as she asked, "What do we do now?"

Before he could reply, the sound of male voices reached him. They couldn't have been more than a few yards away, coming through the woods behind what was left of the mansion, but with his shifter hearing, he could understand them clearly.

"What are we doing back here, man? Perez is dead. There's nothing here."

"This is where we were told to be."

"I know, but why? I don't get it."

Opening his door, Dax slid out of the vehicle, his eyes narrowed on the trees, trying to spot exactly where the men were. Maybe they'd found something that would lead them to Raven after all.

"I'm not questioning the General. I'm just doing what I was told. That's what I get paid for."

"The General said to meet his men here," another voice broke in. "That's all we need to know. We are on his payroll now."

"All I'm saying…"

"You don't get paid to think," a cold, unyielding female voice broke in.

The hair on the back of Dax's neck stood up, and his hand went to the gun at his hip.

"I'm sorry! No, please!"

A gunshot cracked in the air, and there was no doubt in Dax's mind that the person who had been reluctant to meet the man called the General was now dead.

"Rubi, get in the truck," he growled, his eyes trained on the woods. "Now!"

"Sorry. Too late for that."

Dax spun around to see men coming out of trees all around them, their guns raised, pointed at him and his sister.

"I would suggest that you remove your hands from your weapons if you want to live."

Dax stepped back, closer to his sister, his gaze slowly tracking in a circle around the woods.

"Dax," Rubi whispered, closing the distance between them, "who is the General?"

Debating on if he could take them all in dragon form, or if it would be a futile effort, Dax muttered, "I have no idea, but something tells me that our parents might."

He looked into Rubi's stricken eyes as a woman stepped through the trees, walking toward them. "Your father was right, Rubi Dreher. You look almost identical to your sister. The General will love you."

"What do you know about my sister?" Rubi snapped, raising her arm to train her Glock on the woman. "And who the hell are you?"

A slow smile crossed the woman's face, her dark eyes cruel and holding no mercy as she replied, "I'm Ebony. The General is my father. And you, Rubi, are about to be introduced to the hell your sister has been in since we acquired her a year ago." Her eyes straying to Dax, she purred, "Although, I do like your brother." Wetting her lips, she raked her gaze over him, "Maybe I will keep him for myself for a while."

"Fuck you," Dax snarled, sliding his gun from its holster. "You have nothing that interests me, bitch."

"Awe, that's too bad," Ebony said, crossing her arms over her chest and widening her stance. "I guess you will both go to the General, then."

Dax's finger tightened on the trigger, but before he could finish the job, he felt something sharp sink into his neck. Reaching up to yank it out, a low growl vibrated in his chest when he realized it was a tranquilizer dart. He let out a roar when several more imbedded into his skin, and his gun slipped from his fingers, falling uselessly to the ground. His eyes went to Rubi, and he reached out to her, horror filling him at the sight of two darts in her neck, and another in her chest. His legs gave way, and he collapsed, his sister ending up next to him on the hard dirt. He stared into her eyes, watching them flutter, and then slowly drift shut, useless to help her. The last thing he heard was the sound of Ebony's cruel laughter as someone slammed a boot into his gut, and then her order, "Take them to the facility in northern New York. I'm flying in to see my father. I will contact you when I'm ready for you to bring him my…gifts."

6

"Another dead end," Sable growled, crossing the wolf pack in New York off their list. So far, they'd been to Virginia, Delaware, D.C., New Jersey, and now to the first place in New York, without any luck. There was no sign of Aiden and Xavier's sister, nor had she run into the mysterious Dax that Lily spoke of. She couldn't get him off her mind. If Lily was right, and from past experience, there was no doubt in her mind the little girl was, chances that Dax was her mate were high. The thought of someone hurting him was tearing her up inside.

She stiffened when she felt a hand on her shoulder. "We will find him, Sable," Charlotte promised quietly.

Fighting back tears, Sable whispered, "What if we can't? Lily didn't know where he was for sure. Just that he is in trouble." Sighing, she placed the list back in the folder and leaned her head back against the leather seat of her car, before voicing her main concern. "What if it's too late?"

"I don't believe that," Silver said, and Sable could hear the honesty in her words.

"Why not?"

"I've seen people have visions before, Sable. You need to remember everything Lily told you."

Sable's brow furrowed as she glanced back at Silver. "Which part?"

Silver grinned, "She said that Dax will make you happy again, and soon. She also told you not to be afraid of him and his fire. That means two things to me." Sable held her breath while she waited for her friend to continue. "One, you *will* meet him someday, which means that he is not dead."

"And two?"

Silver's eyes lit up with mischief when she said, "Your man is going to be one hot, sexy dragon!"

"Dragon?" Sable whispered in awe, shaking her head slowly. "No, those creatures are a myth. There isn't such a thing as a dragon shifter."

"Are you sure?" Charlotte asked, as she took the folder Sable still held from her. "Just because we've never seen one, doesn't mean they don't exist."

"True, but…dragons?"

"Can you think of any other shifter out there who has fire?" Silver asked, cocking an eyebrow as she leaned closer. "I can't."

"Maybe Dax isn't a shifter," Charlotte said, sifting through the papers on her lap.

"What else would he be?"

"He could be a witch."

Sable's jaw dropped, and Silver laughed as she reached

up and tapped the bottom of her chin. "Whatever he is, the sex is going to be amazing. I mean…fire! I wonder if he has any brothers."

Sable's eyes widened, goosebumps appearing on her skin as she fought back a shiver. Sex with her mate would be amazing no matter who, or what, he was. That was the way it worked. Fate paired all shifters with a mate, someone who held the other half of their soul. And, as far as Sable knew, fate didn't make mistakes. She and Dax would be compatible, in all ways.

"Okay, the next stop is about three hours away," Charlotte interrupted. "I say we find a place to get some food and sleep. Tomorrow we scope out the pack during the day, and then we can hit them late at night if we need to."

Sable wanted to keep going, but she knew Charlotte was right. They needed to eat and get some rest before moving on. The three of them had been pushing hard for close to two weeks now, and they were all exhausted. Still, the need to find Dax was pressing on her, almost suffocating her.

"How about we drive a ways now," Silver suggested, sitting back in her seat. "We can stop a couple of towns over from where we are going. That way, we won't have far to go when we are ready to start stalking our unsuspecting prey."

Sable slid the key into the ignition, glancing into the rear view mirror and letting a small smile slip free at the devilish expression on Silver's face. "Sounds good to me."

"Me, too," Charlotte agreed, slapping her hand on Sable's thigh. "And, I agree with you, Silver. Sex with a fire breathing dragon would be fucking hot! Maybe Dax has two brothers."

Sable couldn't hold back the laughter that bubbled up, even as worry for the man she had still yet to meet consumed her. Putting the car in gear, she vowed to herself that she would not stop until she found him. No matter how long it took.

7

Dax opened his eyes just wide enough to peer through hooded lids. Pain swamped him, and he bit back a groan as he slowly turned his head looking for his little sister. She was chained to an iron post across from him, and didn't seem to be faring any better than he was. The fucking coyote shifters the General's men left them with three days ago beat them on a daily basis, acting as if it were a game to see who could inflict the most pain. One they definitely enjoyed. The only time the agony stopped for him was when he was unconscious, and he knew it was the same for her.

He'd tried to let his dragon out a couple of times, but the bastards shot him with tranquilizer darts every time, effectively stopping his shift. He saw them do the same to Rubi. They were all going to die for what they did to his baby sister. When he got free, and he would if it was the last thing he did, he was going to tear them apart, piece-by-piece.

They were being held in an old barn, surrounded by

trees, out in the middle of nowhere. There were a few houses, no more than small huts, spread out near the barn, but not much else. This was good, because when he was finally able to let his beast free, anyone near him was going to die.

Dax stiffened when he heard the door to their prison open. Seeing his sister's eyelids begin to flutter, he whispered, "Rubi, keep your eyes closed, sis. Someone's coming." To his relief, she seemed to listen, her head lowering slightly, her limp, dirty hair dropping down to hide a portion of her face.

Glancing back toward the door, he watched someone slip inside, and quickly shut the door behind them. It was a woman, petite, with dark brown hair that hung to her waist. She wore a loose, baggy dress that touched her ankles, and her feet were bare. Inhaling deeply, his brow furrowed at the scent of fear that wafted from her. Not only that, but this woman was definitely not a coyote shifter. Not even close. She was a wolf. What the hell was she doing with the fucking mongrels who held him and Rubi?

"Who are you?" Dax demanded roughly, through clenched teeth.

Intent on peering out a small crack in the wood beside the door, the woman jumped, slapping a hand over her mouth to muffle a squeal of surprise as she swung around to look at him. Putting a finger to her lips, she whispered, "Please, you need to be quiet, before someone hears."

She turned back to look through the crack in the wall again, waiting a few more minutes, before quickly crossing the floor to Rubi. Dax bared his teeth at her, growling lowly, "I don't know who you are, but you better get your ass away from my sister."

The woman spared him a glance, before pulling a bottle of water out of her skirt and removing the lid. Holding the bottle to Rubi's lips, she whispered, "Drink." When Rubi raised her head and glared at her, refusing, she gently cupped his sister's jaw in her hand and said, "You have to drink. You both need to be strong so that I can get you out of here before tomorrow night."

"What happens tomorrow night?" Dax snarled.

She looked back at him, the fear evident in her topaz eyes. "The General's men are coming for you. After that, there is nothing I can do." He saw a tear escape as she whispered, "Please, I can't sit back and let them hurt anyone else. I can't watch them send you to your deaths. Please, let me help."

"They will kill you if they find out," Dax said gruffly, the idea of an innocent person's death on his hands not sitting well with him, no matter the reason.

She lifted her head, her steady gaze meeting his. "I would gladly give my life, if it meant you and your sister lived."

Dax stared at her, in awe of her courage even as she trembled before him.

"Dax?"

At his sister's unspoken question, he nodded, and watched Rubi smell the liquid, before opening her mouth and letting the woman help her drink it.

When it was his turn, Dax drank slowly, relishing the feel of it sliding down his dry, aching throat. After he was done, he asked, "What's your name, little one?"

She shrugged, sliding the empty bottle back in her

pocket. "Greta, the woman who watched over me before she died, called me Maya. Everyone else..." she paused, "well, they don't really call me anything."

"Are you a prisoner, too?" Rubi asked softly.

Maya shrugged again, before nodding slowly. "I guess I am, in a way."

"What way?" Dax questioned, trying to figure out how this sweet woman, so willing to give up her life for others, fit in with the coyotes that held them prisoner.

Sighing, Maya ran a hand through her hair, and then wrapped her arms around her waist. "Greta told me that my parents died when I was young, and there was nowhere else for me to go, so she took me in." Taking a deep breath, she whispered, "But, she was lying. I could smell it on her. I have heard others say things when they don't realize I'm around." Swallowing hard, she said, "I was given to them by someone who killed my family. There is no one else out there for me. I'm alone. If I leave, I have nowhere to go."

"You do now," Dax informed her. "When we leave, you will come with us."

Maya shook her head, slowly backing toward the door. "I can't. If they find out, they will hunt you down and kill you. I can't let that happen."

"Why?" Rubi asked. "If you aren't family, why would they care if you left?"

"Because, in their minds, they own me."

"We do own you, wolf," a voice growled, as the door was flung open and the alpha of the coyote pack entered the room. "You aren't going anywhere."

A rough laugh followed as the alpha's mate walked in. "I disagree, Jasper. Greta's gone now, and I'm tired of the bitch. I say we send her to the General with these two." Sliding up next to him, she slipped her arm around his waist and leaned close. "I bet they would give us some money for her. What do you think?"

The alpha threw back his head and laughed, hugging her close. "I like the way your mind works, baby. And, you know I love money." Nodding his head to where Maya stood in shock, he said, "Tie her up and throw her in the back of the truck. She can sit there until Ebony and her men show up tomorrow night."

"What if she runs, Jasper?"

The alpha laughed again. "She ain't going anywhere. She knows better. Don't you girl?"

Maya's eyes widened and she nodded, before quickly lowering her head to the ground. "Yes, sir."

Dax growled, fury filling him at the thought of what Maya was going to endure at the hands of the General for trying to help them.

Jasper grinned, waving a hand to three other coyote shifters who stood nearby. "Show this asshole what happens when a lowlife like him growls at me, boys."

Dax snarled, straining against the chains that held him, his fangs dropping and claws lengthening as he fought to get to the man in front of him.

"What the fuck is he?" someone whispered.

"Who cares? Tranq the bastard and beat the shit out of him!"

Dax roared as he watched one of the men grab Maya and shove her toward the door. She glanced back, tears streaming down her face as she mouthed, 'I'm sorry'. She was shoved again, harder this time, and she stumbled out of the barn, falling to the ground.

Rubi screamed her name, fighting against her bonds, her eyes darkening to a dark ruby red color, before someone yelled, "Tranq her, too! Now!"

"No! Stop!" Maya cried, struggling against the men who held her. "Leave them alone!"

Dax called to his dragon, roaring again in outrage, but it was too late. The darts hit him hard and fast, and within seconds he felt his strength leave him. "Rubi," he whispered, worry for his sister flooding him when he heard her scream in pain, before succumbing to the darkness that called to him.

8

"What the hell?" Charlotte whispered loudly. "Sable, you have to see this," she hissed through their ear coms. "Something's going down, and it doesn't look good."

Sable slid her Beretta into the holster at her waist, and a Glock into the one on her thigh. Grabbing her own binoculars, she quickly threw some loose branches over the top of her car to help hide it from anyone who might drive by. When she was sure it wouldn't be easily spotted, she crossed the road and ran down a small incline into some woods. Making her way to where Charlotte lay on the ground behind some large rocks, she stayed low to the ground to hide her presence from the coyotes in the small town below.

"Shit," Silver growled, from a few feet away. "What are they doing to that poor girl?"

Sable raised her binoculars up to her eyes, adjusting them to zoom in on the scene in front of her. There was an old, piece of shit barn below, surrounded by what looked like several small houses. Maybe ten of them. Readjusting the focus on her binoculars, she caught her breath when she saw a young woman fall to her knees in front of the barn door, and then gasped when a loud roar split through the air. The girl struggled to her feet, reaching toward the barn, but a large man with a tattoo sleeve on one arm backhanded her, and she fell again. She seemed to be pleading with someone inside the building, but the people around her just laughed.

Another loud roar, full of fury, echoed through the woods, and Sable's hands tightened on the binoculars. "Dax," she rasped, somehow knowing it was him. As she watched, a man rounded the side of the barn with a baseball bat in his hand, followed by another with what looked like a pipe wrench. She saw their intentions clearly written in the expressions, and fear filled her.

When Sable would have risen to go to the man she believed to be her mate, she felt an arm go around her back, pinning her to the ground. "Wait," Charlotte whispered quietly. "Running off half-cocked isn't the answer." When a soft whimper left Sable's throat at the thought of leaving him down there to suffer at the hands of the coyotes who held him, Charlotte tightened her hold, murmuring, "I know, my friend. But, running into that camp without a plan could get not only him killed, but us, too."

"He's strong," Silver said quietly through the coms. "He will make it until we can get to him."

Sable nodded, knowing it was true, even if she hated the fact that she couldn't save him now. She bit her lip hard, drawing blood, as she watched the men enter the barn, the first one raising his bat with a sneer as he yelled, "Miss me, motherfucker? You want some more of this?"

Her breaths came in small pants as she tried to control her wolf, who wanted to rush down the side of the hill they were hiding on and rip the bastard's head off. Sable moaned, grasping her binoculars so hard she heard the casing crack. "I'm going to kill them," she vowed quietly. "I'm going to hurt them, like they are hurting him. I am going to make them suffer, and then I am going to tear out their fucking throats."

"We will be right there with you, girl," Silver promised, her own wolf evident in her voice. "No one below who has taken part in what is going on with that young girl and your mate will survive this night."

Closing her eyes, Sable took a deep breath, and then another, trying to calm the raging fury flowing through her. When she was sure she was under control, she opened them again, and whispered, "I'm fine."

"No, you aren't," Charlotte replied, letting her go and moving back to her original position, "but I trust you not to rush into their camp and blow our cover now."

Sable didn't bother to respond as she looked back down below and watched one of the assholes haul the young woman back to her feet, and someone else wrap a thick piece of rope around her wrists, tying her hands together. He growled something at her, and she reared back, spitting in his face. The man struck out, slamming his fist into the side of her head, and then kicking her hard in the stomach when she fell to the ground. "Dammit," Sable swore lowly, wishing there was something she could do.

"Stop fighting, sweetheart," Silver whispered.

As she watched, the girl lay still, not moving. The man yanked her up off the ground and swung her around, pushing her toward a truck that was a couple of yards from the barn. Sable gasped when she got her first real look at the girl's face. "It's her," she said softly, zooming in until the small features were clearer.

"Who?"

"Aiden and Xavier's sister."

"No way," Charlotte muttered. "How do you know?"

"Look closely," Sable murmured, her eyes never leaving the girl's face as she was shoved again. "The eyes, the nose, the shape of the mouth."

"Holy shit!" Silver exclaimed excitedly in a low voice, "You're right. She looks just like the twins!"

"Seriously, what are the odds?" Charlotte said suspiciously. "Your mate and their sister in the same place? That can't be a coincidence, can it?"

Sable watched until the girl was thrown in the back of the truck, and left there alone, before slowly canvasing the area.

"They didn't bother to tie her legs," Silver muttered.

"What?" she asked distractedly as her gaze stopped on the front of the barn where a man and woman were walking through the door.

"The girl. They tied her hands together, but not her ankles. For some reason, they don't think she will make a run for it."

"Because she won't," Charlotte murmured. "Think about it. She was obviously trying to save Dax. She won't just leave him there."

Sable nodded in agreement, even though she knew her friends couldn't see her. Charlotte was right. The girl wouldn't have risked her life to save someone, just to leave them there to die.

"So, boss lady," Silver drawled, "what are we going to do?"

What were they going to do? The answer to that was simple. "When darkness falls, we are getting them both the hell out of there."

TEN HOURS LATER, while most of the coyote pack was asleep, Sable slipped into the camp, Charlotte and Silver on her heels. As much as she wanted to head straight for the barn and Dax, Sable went to the truck first. Her team crouched low in the darkness, one on each side, standing watch while she slid into the back of the truck bed where the woman sat huddled in the front corner.

Sable saw the girl's eyes widen and her mouth open, and she just managed to clamp a hand over her mouth before the scream could emerge. "Shhh, I'm here to help," she whispered softly. "You need to stay quiet so that we can get you out of here."

The girl shook her head frantically, trying to speak against Sable's hand. Sable let up slightly, and she gasped, "No, we have to help them. I can't leave them here."

"I have no plans to leave without Dax," Sable assured her quietly.

"They have his sister, too," the woman whispered. "We have to take them both."

Sable stared in surprise, but then nodded, "Of course. They will both come with us."

"Wait, who are you?"

Sable smiled gently, removing her hand fully from the woman's mouth. "I'm a friend of your brothers. My alpha sent me to find you, and bring you home."

"Brothers?"

She saw the shock and denial in the woman's eyes, but they didn't have time for it right now. "I will tell you about them later, but right now, we need to get Dax and his sister, and get the hell out of here."

Not waiting for a reply, Sable tugged on the woman's arm, urging her to move to the back of the truck where Charlotte was now waiting to help her down. "Where's Silver?"

Charlotte's gaze tracked around the area as she whispered, "A guy showed up at the wrong time to take a leak. She's handling it."

"I'm here now," Silver said, appearing beside them. "Let's do this."

Placing the woman between them, Sable in the lead, they skirted across the distance from the truck to the barn and slipped inside.

9

Dax gritted his teeth against the throbbing pain on his left side, positive the bastards had cracked a rib this time. His entire body screamed out in agony, but he was pretty sure that was the worst of it. Lifting his head, he looked over at his sister, surprised to see her staring back at him, her eyes dark with anger.

"I'm done, brother. That is the last time they are going to hurt us like that."

"You got that right," a female voice snapped in a low, husky tone from the entrance of the barn. "The next time one of those fucking wanna be dogs touches my mate, I'm going to feed their balls to them."

"Damn, Sable," another voice drawled, as four women came into view, "meeting Dax for the first time is supposed to be a happy occasion."

Dax's eyes fell on the dark haired beauty standing in front of the others, his dick hardening when her scent reached him. His dragon roared in his mind, recognizing his mate instantly, and Dax tugged weakly on the chains that held him as his gaze raked over her. She was tall and slender, with black hair that stopped just past her shoulders, and hazel eyes that were bright with anger as they roamed over him, taking in the dark bruises that covered his body and slices carved into his flesh. "I'm sure he will be happy to watch me kill the bastards who did this to him and his sister," she growled.

One of the women chuckled softly, crossing the room to where Rubi stared at them. "We can debate this later. Right now, I say we get the hell out of here."

"I have no idea who any of you are, but I agree," Rubi responded, tugging on the chains that held her.

"They came to save us," Maya said, slipping out from behind one of them.

"Maya," Rubi gasped, "are you okay?"

Dax couldn't seem to pull his eyes away from the woman in front of him. The one they called Sable. She was stunning, in a pair of dark jeans, a black shirt that clung to her figure, and a black leather jacket. He had found her, after all this time. His mate.

"Yes," Maya said, taking a step toward Rubi, "but we have to hurry."

Suddenly, there was a noise outside the barn and Dax snapped back to awareness, a low growl building in his chest at the thought of someone threatening his beautiful mate. "Hide," he ordered darkly, his gaze going to the door.

"Awe, sugar, you don't know us very well," the woman who stood beside Sable teased. "We don't hide for anyone."

Sable took a step toward him, her eyes darkening as she slipped a knife from her boot. As he watched, she bared her teeth and growled, "Silver, Charlotte, get them out of those chains. I'll take care of whoever's come to visit."

The women instantly responded, moving to work on the locks that held Dax and Rubi, while his fearless mate turned to face the danger behind her.

"Sable," Dax growled, hating the thought of his woman in danger.

"Don't you worry about her, sugar," the woman kneeling beside him drawled as she picked at the locking mechanism. "You just let her take out the trash while we get you out of these things."

His eyes never left his mate as he strained against the chains that held him, his dragon rising to the surface, fighting to take over. Sable palmed a knife in one hand and a gun in the other, a low growl rumbling in her throat as she turned to meet the threat of two men who walked through the door. One held a baseball bat, another a large pipe wrench.

"Boy, I am one lucky girl," Sable drawled, when the men finally noticed her. "I was hoping I would get to meet both of you."

"Oh yeah?" one of them asked, hitting the bat in the palm of his hand as he closed the distance between them.

"Who the fuck are you?" the other one snarled, following close behind.

Ignoring the second one, Sable slipped her gun back into her pocket, and slid another knife out of her boot. "Yeah," she said, taking a step toward them, and then pausing slightly. "I saw you earlier today, and knew exactly what I was going to do when we met."

"Who are you?" the second one demanded again.

Dax watched as Sable slowly walked in a circle around the men until she was on the other side, facing him. Then, her eyes met his and she growled, "I'm the woman who is about to rock your world, gentleman. Too bad you won't live to talk about it, but that's what you get for fucking with my mate."

Before they could respond, Sable stepped between the two of them, bringing one of her daggers up and deftly slicing through the neck of the one who held the baseball bat. When it fell to the floor so he could grasp at the wound with both hands, she kicked it away and turned to the other one. Dax was sure he didn't know what hit him when she plunged her other knife deep into his heart, before grasping his neck and twisting it hard. There was an audible crack, and then she dropped his lifeless body to the floor. "Not the slow, painful death I wanted for you bastards, but this will have to do."

Dax felt his chains fall away, and he stumbled forward, stopping just inches from the gorgeous woman in front of him. She was amazing, and he wanted nothing more than to sink balls deep into her and claim her right then. Unfortunately, that wasn't going to happen. They needed to leave before more people arrived to check on them. Afterwards, he still needed to find Raven. As much as he wanted to claim the stunning creature before him, it wasn't going to happen just yet.

"We need to go," she whispered, reaching out to cup his jaw in the palm of her hand.

Dax nodded, fighting a wave a dizziness that threatened to put him on his knees. He felt her arm slide around his waist, and then the woman came up beside him offering her help as well. "This has been a lot of fun, but I think it's time we get the hell out of here," she said. "We need to get Maya home."

"No," Rubi protested weakly as Maya helped her make her way over to them, "we can't leave. Not until we find Raven."

"Raven?" Sable asked with a frown, her gaze going from him to Rubi.

"My other sister," he told her. "Rubi and I were looking for her when that bitch, Ebony, grabbed us."

Sable stiffened, her face flushing a dark red in anger. "Ebony? The General's daughter?"

"You know who he is?" Rubi asked hopefully. "He has our sister. We need to get her back."

Sable sighed, motioning toward the door. "Yes, we know who he is. Let's get out of here and go somewhere we can talk. I need to call my alpha and fill him in on what happened here, and then we need to come up with a plan."

"A plan?" Rubi whispered, her eyes filling with tears. "You mean, you are going to help us?"

Sable looked up at him, briefly touching his cheek again before looking over at his sister. "Of course, I am. Dax is my mate, which makes you and Raven my family. And I am getting pretty damned tired of the General fucking with my family."

"I'm in," both of Sable's friends growled at the same time.

She looked at them, smiling gratefully. "Let's go contact Chase and Angel. They will want to be in on this."

Dax's grip on his mate tightened, and he stared down

at her, trying to figure out how he had gotten so damn lucky. When she looked up, meeting his eyes, he couldn't resist dropping a small kiss on her lips before moving toward the door. Somehow, he would keep her safe, along with Rubi, and they would find Raven. He wanted that promise of a future he saw in her eyes. He needed it.

10

Deciding that staying in New York was too great of a risk with both Dax and Rubi injured, Sable drove until early in the morning when she hit Pennsylvania, finally stopping at a rundown hotel in a small town out in the middle of nowhere. Dax sat beside her, his head resting against the back of the seat, his hand clutching tightly to hers, even in sleep. Rubi and Maya were in the back between Charlotte and Silver, also asleep. It was a tight fit, but somehow they made it work.

Pulling into the parking lot, Sable stopped near the front door. "I'm going to see if they have a room available," she said softly, her eyes on her team in the rear view mirror. "Silver, shift and do a perimeter sweep, going out at least a mile around us. Make sure we weren't followed. Charlotte, keep my family safe until I get back."

She felt Dax squeeze her hand, and she glanced over at him. Sable caught her breath at the look in his eyes, a shiver running up her spine. "Get two rooms," he said gruffly. When she hesitated, he growled, "I want to spend some time alone with my mate."

A jolt of pure lust shot through her, from her clit straight to her sensitive nipples. Dax inhaled, and his eyes began to glow a bright green. She ran her gaze down over his bare chest, and lower to where she could see his thick erection straining against what was left of his jeans.

"Dax, you need to heal," she told him, trying to tug her hand from his. As much as she wanted what the look in his eyes was promising, the dark bruises covering his skin, along with the look of pain that he couldn't hide etched into his face, said now was not the time. She didn't want to do anything else that would hurt him.

"I know what I need," Dax growled, licking his lips as his eyes went to her chest where her beaded nipples were clearly showing, before rising back to meet her gaze. "But, for now, I just want to hold you and talk."

Sable nodded slowly, "Okay, but first I need to contact my alpha."

"Agreed."

With one last look at him, Sable slid from the car and let Silver out. "Be safe," she murmured to the wolf, before heading to the front door.

Fifteen minutes later, they had two rooms beside each other, but were all sitting in one while they waited for Silver to return.

"We need to get some food," Sable told Charlotte quietly, her eyes on Rubi who lay on one of the beds. Dax sat beside her with his back resting against the headboard. Rubi's eyes were closed, and soft snores filled the air, but she clutched a dagger that Silver had given her in the car tightly in her hand. Dax looked as if he was asleep, but

Sable knew better. She could practically feel the tension surrounding him. "They need to get their strength up, quickly."

"We passed some golden arches a couple of miles back. Want me to grab some burritos and biscuits?"

"I can go with her," Maya volunteered from where she lay on the other bed, fighting against her own exhaustion.

Sable shook her head, "They will be looking for you, Maya. You need to stay out of sight." She tossed Charlotte the keys to the car, sliding her Glock from the holster on her thigh. "Take Silver with you when she comes back. Rubi can rest awhile longer. She's hurting something fierce. I can smell her pain."

Charlotte nodded, crossing to the door and slipping outside. Once she was gone, Dax rasped, "You think there's something wrong with my sister?"

Sable palmed her Glock and walked over to the window, sliding the curtain back slightly so she could look outside. "Yes, I do."

"Why wouldn't she say anything?"

Sable let a small smile appear as she glanced back at him. "Because she's like me. If I'm on a mission, I don't care how badly I'm injured, I don't stop until the job is done."

"Rubi doesn't go on missions."

"She's on one now, Dax. A very important one." Sable's eyes falling to Rubi's pale cheeks with dark circles under her eyes, she whispered, "And she has a lot to lose this time."

"Raven."

Sable nodded, her gaze going to the window. "There is nothing like the bond of a twin. They share a very special relationship, one that you can't understand unless you are a twin yourself."

"How do you know?"

Sable was silent for a moment, her eyes on the trees beyond the hotel. When Silver emerged, she met Charlotte by the car, and then gave Sable a thumbs up. Sighing, Sable slid her Glock back in the holster and turned to face her mate. "Because, my best friend is a twin. He and his brother are inseparable. They do almost everything together, and it's almost as if they know each other's thoughts. They have their own unique personalities, but there is a bond there that no one will ever break."

"Just like me and Raven," Rubi whispered, her eyes fluttering open. "I feel so…so empty without her. Like I'm not whole. I miss her so much."

"The pain you are feeling at losing your sister, is nothing compared to what Rubi is feeling, Dax," Sable said softly.

Dax ran a hand down Rubi's hair, and then settled it on her shoulder. "I didn't know, sis."

A tear slipped out, tracking its way down Rubi's cheek. She grasped Dax's hand tightly in hers, whispering, "I know."

"Are you in a lot of pain, Rubi?" Dax asked quietly. "Sable thinks something might be wrong."

Rubi didn't respond right away. Finally, she nodded. "Yes."

Sable crossed the room and sat on the bed beside her. "Do you think it would help if you shifted?"

Another tear slipped free as Rubi shook her head. "I can't. It hurts too much."

Dax swore softly, raking a hand through his hair. "We have to get her to a doctor, Sable."

"No! Raven needs us, Dax. We can't leave her with that bastard!" Huge sobs began to shake her body, and she clutched her stomach as she cried out in pain.

"We aren't going to leave her," Sable soothed, running a hand gently down her arm. "I promise, we won't leave her there. I have friends who can help. Friends who hate the General, and who will stop at nothing until he is brought down."

"We have to find her, Sable. Please, we have to bring her home."

"We will," Sable promised, "but you are in no shape to do anything right now. I'm going to call my alpha, and see if he can get a plane out here to pick us up. You need a doctor, Rubi."

"I don't want to leave here. I feel like we are getting close to finding Raven. What if he moves her?"

"If you don't see a doctor, you may not live to rescue your sister," Sable said bluntly.

"It's not life threatening," Rubi argued. "I would know if it was. I'm just in a lot of pain."

"Call your alpha," Dax cut in.

"But, Dax!"

Dax gently cupped Rubi's cheek in his hand, wiping away the tears that still streamed down her face. "We get you fixed first, and then we go after Raven. You aren't going to do her any good like this, sprite."

Anger seeped into Rubi's eyes, and she snapped, "Well, it better not take too long, Dax, or I'm going to light your ass on fire!"

Dax chuckled, leaning down to place a kiss on her head. "There's my Rubi. Feisty and bold."

Sable saw him flinch as he pushed himself back up to lean against the headboard again. She slowly traced his chest with her eyes, taking in the dark purple and blue bruises. He had to be in so much pain himself, but all he seemed to worry about was his sister. Fury filled her at the thought of what he must have gone through before she got to him. It made her want to go back to the coyote camp and kill them all for hurting her mate. Dammit, she should have been there for him. She should have been able to prevent it from happening.

"Sable?" Dax said her name softly, breaking through her thoughts, and bringing her back to the present. "What's wrong?"

Sable rose from the bed, clenching her hands tightly into fists as she met his eyes. "I need to call Chase." She couldn't tell him how she had failed. That she knew he was out there, that she'd tried to find him to prevent the hell she knew he was going to go through, but she hadn't been able to.

"Sable, talk to me."

"Not right now." Sable slipped her phone from her pocket and dialed Chase's number. It only rang twice before he answered. "I need your help, Alpha," she said quietly.

"I'm here."

"I have Maya."

"Maya?"

"Aiden and Xavier's sister. She was with the coyote shifters in New York."

"How is she?"

Sable's gaze went to the young woman who lay on her side, her eyes closed in sleep. "Physically, she seems fine, except for being slightly malnourished. Mentally, I'm not sure."

She heard Chase sighed deeply, and then he growled, "Bring her home, Sable. We will make sure she gets the care she needs." When she didn't reply right away, Chase asked, "Was there something else?"

Sable swallowed hard, her eyes meeting Dax's before she said, "I found him."

"Him?"

"My mate. Lily was right."

Chase was silent for a moment, before asking, "Do I need to send backup?"

Sable's hand tightened on the phone, and her heart warmed at her alpha's gesture. Once again, he had proven that he would do anything for the people in his pack. Instead of grilling her about Dax, he'd offered his help first. Turning from her mate's questioning gaze, Sable crossed the room to look out the window. "I was hoping you would send a plane to pick up Maya and Dax's sister, Rubi. The coyotes were holding Dax and Rubi captive. Beating them. Something is wrong with Rubi, but I'm not sure what. She's in a lot of pain, and can't shift to help with healing."

Chase swore softly, "I wish I could, Sable, but Angel has the jet. She went to look for Jeremiah, and they've gone dark. I have no way of contacting her right now."

"That's another thing we need to discuss," Sable murmured. "The General."

"Talk to me," Chase growled.

"He has Dax and Rubi's sister." Sable hesitated, before continuing, "I promised them we would help find her."

"That son of a bitch," Chase snarled. "I am sick and tired of him fucking with our pack."

Sable's eyes flew to Dax, and she whispered, "Our pack?"

"Dax is your mate," Chase growled, "that makes him and his sisters pack. Unless, they are already part of a pack they don't want to leave. Which, I hope they aren't, because I don't want to lose you, Sable."

"You aren't going to lose me," Sable promised, knowing there was no other pack she would want to be a part of. No other alphas her wolf would accept except for Chase and Angel.

"We are dragons," Dax said quietly. "We don't have packs. And, even if we did, I would never ask you to leave yours."

"Dragons?" Chase asked, and Sable could hear the shock in his voice. He obviously could hear Dax, just as Dax could hear his side of the conversation. Damn, shifter hearing.

Pushing the speaker button on her phone to make it easier for Dax to listen, she responded, "Yes, Alpha, Dax and his sisters are dragons."

"Damn. I'd heard rumors that dragons were real, but I've never actually come across one before."

"Our king likes us to keep in the shadows as much as possible. He wants to keep our existence from people who would use it against us."

"Like the General."

"Correct."

"Will you really help us find Raven?" Rubi asked, pushing herself up to sit against the headboard.

"Of course, I will," Chase told her. "That's what pack does."

Rubi looked up at Dax, and then over at Sable. "You accept us because Sable is my brother's mate?"

"I accept you because Sable does," was Chase's quiet response. "She is one of mine, to care for and protect. You are now her family, which means that protection is extended to you, whether you choose to become a part of our pack or not."

"Thank you, Alpha," Dax said gruffly.

"Tell me about Raven."

For the next few minutes, Dax and Rubi relayed their story to Chase, and Sable sat in silence, her heart going out to them. Raven's sister had been sold by her parents to Philip Perez, Trace's now deceased father. The bastards. What kind of parent sold their own flesh and blood? Afterwards, it sounded as if the General bought their sister from Perez. He'd had her for a year or so now, so who knew what the crazy maniac had already done to her.

Charlotte and Silver arrived in the middle of the story, and quietly handed out food, before taking a seat at the table in the corner to eat their own breakfast.

"I know that you all want to go after Raven right now, and I don't blame you, but you can't do that on your own," Chase finally said, once Dax and Rubi were finished. "Sable, your first priority is to bring Maya and Rubi home. After that, we will devise a plan to go after Raven. We can't go in half-cocked. It won't do anyone any good, and it will probably cost lives."

"With all due respect, Alpha," Dax interjected, "I will be staying behind."

"Dax, no!" Rubi whispered, grasping his hand tightly. "We stay together!"

"The General's daughter is supposed to be coming back to the camp tonight to get us. I intend to be waiting. I'm going to follow her and see if she leads me to Raven."

While it sounded like a good plan, Sable wasn't about to let her mate stay behind by himself. "If you stay, I stay," she growled, her eyes going wolf.

11

Dax had never seen anything as sexy as his mate right at that moment. Her eyes seemed to glow, and he could just barely see the tips of her fangs. Fangs he wanted buried deep inside his shoulder, claiming him. She was beautiful, fierce, protective, and he fought back a groan as his dick began to harden in his pants. Slipping from the bed, he walked to the door, grabbing the key for the other room off the dresser on his way by. "I need a shower."

"Dax, we need to talk about this."

There was no way in hell he was going to stay in that room with his mate and four other women while his cock was hard as a rock. He wanted to be alone with Sable. "I'll be in our room when you are ready to talk," he growled, a shudder running through him when her tongue snuck out, licking her bottom lip.

"Dax." The alpha's voice stopped him in his tracks, and he waited for the man to continue, his hand on the doorknob. "My mate is the leader of an elite mercenary group, and is often gone on long missions. During that time, I may speak to her once or twice, if that. It's harder than fuck, man. I want to be there, helping her, protecting her, even though I know she is very capable of taking care of herself." Chase paused, "I can't go with her, Dax, because I have responsibilities here. My pack needs me."

Dax bowed his head and nodded. Then, realizing the other man couldn't see him, he replied, "Point taken, Alpha," before opening the door and walking out of the room.

SABLE WATCHED DAX GO, wanting nothing more than to follow him, but she needed to finish her conversation with Chase first. "I will send Charlotte and Silver home with Maya and Rubi."

"Sable, I don't want to leave my brother," Rubi whispered, tears filling her eyes. "I've already lost my sister. I can't lose Dax."

"You aren't going to," Sable vowed softly, walking over to sit on the bed beside her. Covering Rubi's hand with her own, she smiled, "I don't care what my dragon says, I'm not leaving his side."

Rubi nodded, swiping at her tears. "Thank you."

"Send the others in your car, Sable, and rent another one for the time being. I'll have Angel and her team fly out to meet you as soon as they get back."

"Thank you, Alpha."

Ending the call, Sable squeezed Rubi's hand before rising. Glancing at her watch, she said, "I'll take first watch. Get some rest."

"Like that is going to happen," Silver snickered, crinkling up the wrapper from her breakfast burrito and tossing it into the trash. "Go to your mate, Sable. Charlotte and I will handle this."

"You have a long drive ahead of you," Sable argued, knowing by the look in her friend's eyes that it was a losing battle.

"I slept on the way here. You didn't." When Sable would have argued again, Silver held up a hand, "Sable, go. We got this. I promise."

Sable glanced around the room, her gaze falling on the sleeping women on the beds. One, the sister of her best friend. The other, the sister of her mate. She would give her life for either of them in a heartbeat. Nodding, she ordered darkly, "Keep them safe. If anyone comes in this room except for me or Dax, shoot them."

Charlotte rose, crossing the room to give her a hug. "We will keep them safe. Promise."

Giving her a quick hug in return, Sable murmured, "Thank you, both." With one last glance at the women, Sable left the room.

Opening the door next to it, she made sure to lock it behind her before taking in the empty room. This one had a king-sized bed, but other than that, it was identical to the one the others were in...except for the pair of torn up jeans that lay on the floor in front of the bathroom. Her mouth went dry at the thought of Dax naked.

Slowly, she removed her weapons and placed them on the nightstand beside the bed. Then, she began to peel off her own clothes. The shower was running, and she could just imagine the water sliding over Dax's skin, delicious beads of moisture for her to lick off. She wanted to run her tongue over every inch of his hard body. They may have just met, but they were mates. The instant attraction was there, as was the need to complete their mate bond. It pushed at her, making a soft growl emerge from her throat. Dax was hers, and she wanted him. She may not know everything there was to know about her dragon just yet, but they would have many years to figure all of that out. Fate had chosen them as mates, and She didn't make mistakes. No matter what, this man was hers, and she wasn't waiting until they got back home to claim him.

12

Dax ran the soap over his body, reveling in how good it felt to finally be clean again. Removing the stench of the coyotes who worked him over in that barn, made his dragon happy. Even though Sable killed them, his dragon wanted to go back and rip their heads off after what they did to him and Rubi. Getting rid of the smell helped his animal calm down, and the thing was practically purring in the back of his mind now.

His body was sore, but with his increased healing abilities, he was already starting to feel better. Dax knew if he could shift a couple of times, he would be good as new. Unfortunately, he wouldn't be able to do that anytime soon. His dragon was huge, and he couldn't risk anyone seeing it.

Sliding the bar of soap down over his abs, he quickly cleaned his cock that was still hard as hell. Unable to stop himself, he wrapped his hand around it, groaning as the scent of his mate filled the bathroom. He couldn't get her out of his mind. Fuck, he needed her.

Stepping back from the showerhead, Dax leaned against the wall and began to pump his hips, his wet, soap slicked dick moving easily in his hand. Sable's name slipped from his lips as he moved, closing his eyes to concentrate on an image of her as he struggled to find a quick release to take the edge off.

"Mine!"

Dax's eyes flew open, and he froze, his gaze going to the sexy woman who pulled back the shower curtain and stepped in, closing it again. "Sable." Her name was a rough groan on his lips.

"Mine," she growled again, pulling his hand away from his dick.

His gaze raked over her, taking in the smooth skin he wanted to lick, round, pert breasts he wanted to fill his hands with, and her slender waist, with the triangle of dark curls below it. His mouth began to water at the thought of what those dark curls hid from him. "Need you," he rasped, a shudder running through his body at the sight before him.

As he watched, his mate lowered herself to her knees, her gaze never leaving his as she leaned forward and ran her tongue over the tip of his cock. "You will have me," she promised huskily, "but first, I want to taste you."

A low growl worked its way up his throat when Sable traced her tongue along the side of his dick, and then licked around the head, before engulfing him in her hot, wet mouth. "Fuck!"

Sable began to move up and down his cock, sucking him deep, and then slowly letting him go, before doing it all over again. Cupping his balls, she tugged gently on them as she sank her nails into his ass. Water flowed over her head, sliding down her cheeks and below, cascading over her breasts.

The sight of her lips encasing his dick nearly drove him mad, and it wasn't long before Dax sank his fingers into her soft, silky hair and took over, loving the feel of her mouth surrounding him. "Baby, you are so fucking hot," he snarled, increasing his pace, his gaze going to her shoulder as his fangs punched through his gums. He saw Sable's eyes widen, and knew it was because his incisors were much longer than other shifters. "Won't hurt you," he promised raggedly through gritted teeth, knowing he probably looked feral at the moment. His need to claim her was driving him wild, and there was nothing he could do to stop it. His dragon was pushing hard at him to take her and make her his.

Dax saw nothing but trust and desire in her captivating eyes. When she let go of his balls and ran her nails down the back of his leg, he tightened his hold in her hair, pushing into her mouth again. Finally, he could take no more, and he pulled himself free of the heaven her mouth was, lifting her up and turning her around to place her back against the wall.

"I need you, Sable," Dax rasped, rubbing his straining cock against her thigh. "If you don't want this, you need to tell me now."

"I want you," she moaned, wrapping her legs around his waist. "Please, Dax."

"If I take you, Sable, I will claim you. And I will never let you go. If you need more time, now's the time to say something."

He watched her eyes begin to glow, and she smiled, showing off her fangs. "I came into this bathroom with the intention of claiming you, Dax, and I am not leaving until I do."

Dax growled, grasping the firm globes of her ass in his hands, and lifting her slightly until his cock found her entrance that he craved. His gaze on hers, he slowly pushed inside her, his hands tightening on her skin when he was suddenly surrounded by wet heat. It felt even better than he'd imagined, and he had to fight not to come inside her right then.

"Move," Sable ordered, clutching his shoulders as she adjusted her hips and began to ride his cock. "Make me feel you, Dax."

Another low growl rose from his chest, sliding up his throat as he began to pump his hips, moving deep inside her. "Mine," he snarled, his hips going faster and faster as small flames began to appear, rolling over his skin.

Sable's eyes widened, but she didn't pull back in fear. "Your fire," she gasped, running a hand down his arm, through the flames.

"Won't hurt you," he grunted, his gaze going to her shoulder. "Dragon fire never hurts a mate."

Sable raked her nails over his shoulders, tilting her head back as she moaned, "I know you won't hurt me, Dax. But, if you don't sink your fangs into me soon, I'm going to hurt you!"

Not needing any further invitation, Dax shoved deep inside her one last time, roaring as he came, right before clamping down on her shoulder and embedding his teeth deep into her skin.

Sable cried out, stilling in his arms, and then leaning forward and biting into his shoulder as she came around him. "Mine," she panted, not letting go. "Mine."

Dax had never felt anything like it. It was as if they were suddenly one, fate binding their souls together, merging them into one whole being. He stood there, his cock jerking in his mate, his fangs deep in her shoulder, and he had never felt more whole in his life.

After several moments, he finally removed his fangs, and licked over the mating bite, groaning when Sable did the same. The feeling of his mate's tongue stroking over the mark where she'd just claimed him made him want to take her again.

Fighting the urge, knowing they still had a lot to discuss, he kissed her softly before turning her around. Retrieving the soap from the bottom of the tub, he slowly washed her. After quickly cleaning himself, Dax shut off the water and opened the curtain. It didn't take long to dry them both off, and then he scooped his exhausted mate in his arms and took her into the next room, gently laying her on the bed and crawling in behind her. Lying on his back, he tugged Sable over and onto his chest, catching his breath slightly at the dull ache that followed. His mate had managed to make him forget about his pain for a while. Holding her close, he whispered, "No matter what happens, Sable, I am so glad fate brought us together, and I am honored to be your mate."

She looked up at him with her big, hazel eyes, and whispered, "Me, too," as she cupped his cheek in her hand. "Dax, I'm so sorry I didn't find you in time." Her gaze lowered to his chest, and a tear slipped free, trailing down her face. "I tried, I really did, but I didn't know anything about you except that your first name was Dax."

"Sweetheart, what are you talking about? How could you have known about me?"

Sable bit her lip, swallowing hard, before whispering, "I'm going to tell you something, but you have to promise to keep it a secret. You can't tell anyone."

Seeing how much it meant to her, Dax nodded, "I give you my word as a dragon warrior." When she frowned, he gently traced her cheek with the tip of his finger. "I've been training to be a warrior all of my life, and spent the past ten years as a dragon warrior to our king. No one is more honest and loyal than a dragon warrior. Our word is our bond. No matter what you tell me, I will not share it, even upon death."

Her eyes widening, Sable nodded slowly, before leaning up to give him a soft kiss. Dax groaned, taking control and covering her mouth with his. He traced her lips with his tongue, then slipped past them to tangle it with hers, swallowing her moan of pleasure. He felt his cock begin to harden again, but made himself pull back. Resting his forehead on hers, he rasped, "We better get through this talk fast, because I want nothing more than to sink inside you again, beautiful mate."

Sable's eyes lit with desire, and she nodded, kissing him one last time before laying her head tentatively on his chest. "Am I hurting you?"

"No," he whispered, loving the way she felt in his arms. Running a hand slowly up and down her back, he said, "I'm healing fast, sweetheart. I will be fine soon."

Sable sighed, snuggling closer. "Good." He waited patiently for her to continue, and after a few moments she whispered, "I know some people who have certain…gifts. Some speak telepathically to each other, some see into the future, things like that."

When Sable paused, as if unsure he would believe her,

Dax replied, "Once a dragon warrior takes the oath to serve the king, during that time, they can speak telepathically to each other."

"You can do that?" Sable asked in surprise, looking up at him.

Dax grinned, shaking his head, "I could when I was part of the king's elite dragons, but now that I have resigned, I don't have the ability anymore. And, it only worked with each other. I wouldn't have been able to talk to you."

Sable nodded, once again lowering her head to his chest. "Well, not many know this, but my alpha's niece has the ability to see into the future. I saw her right before I left, and she told me about you. She said I was going to meet someone who would make me smile again. He would make me happy."

"Wait," Dax interrupted, slipping a finger under her chin and raising her head until their eyes met. "What does that mean, Sable? Why were you unhappy in the first place?"

He felt Sable stiffen next to him, then she lowered her eyes, refusing to meet his gaze. "Do you really want to know?"

"I wouldn't have asked if I didn't," he told her gently. "Tell me, sweetheart."

She licked her lips, then whispered, "I thought I loved someone, Dax. Someone who I knew didn't return my feelings. I was wrong. My feelings for him were nothing more than friendship, maybe even that of a brother, but I didn't realize it then. It was hard on me being around him all of the time."

Dax ran a hand gently down her hair, waiting patiently

until she finally raised her eyes to meet his. "As much as I don't like the thought of you caring about any other man but me, I understand."

"You do?"

"I'm forty-five years old, Sable. I haven't exactly been celibate all my life."

"You're mine," Sable growled, her eyes snapping in anger.

Dax laughed, kissing her gently before saying, "Yes, I am. As you are mine. Even if fate hadn't already chosen for us, I would choose you, Sable. You can tell me anything. Anything. It won't change how I feel about you."

Tears filled Sable's eyes and she whispered, "Lily told me that I had to hurry. That you were going to be captured and they were going to hurt you." Tears streamed down her face as she cried, "I knew you were out there somewhere. That someone was going to capture you and torture you, but there wasn't a damn thing I could do about it. All I had was a name, and Lily is just a seven-year-old child. She didn't have any more details for me. I'm so sorry, Dax. I should have found you sooner. I should have stopped you and Rubi from being hurt."

"Baby, stop," Dax ordered, sliding down in the bed so they were face to face. "There was nothing you could have done, Sable. Nothing. I'm here now. I'm alive, and so is my sister. You saved us, sweetheart! You walked into the barn, took out the men who hurt us, and saved us."

Sobs tore from his mate's throat, and he pulled her tight against him, rubbing his hands over her body to try and calm her.

"But, they tortured you!"

Dax cupped her cheek in his hand and leaned down,

capturing her lips with his, groaning when she pushed into him. He loved the way she tasted, and how she responded so quickly to his touch. Breathing heavily, he pulled back just enough to rasp, "I would go through it a million times just to be where I am right now, at this moment. I would do anything to have you in my arms, Sable. You are everything to me."

Sable pressed her mouth to his again, and he slipped his tongue past her lips, into the hot recesses of her mouth. Rolling her over onto her back, he slid deep inside her, and began jacking his hips first slowly, then faster and faster. He loved the way she felt, loved so many things about this woman.

"Please, Dax," she cried, matching him thrust for thrust as she clung to him. "Oh, God!"

Knowing he wasn't going to last long, not with the way Sable was moving under him, Dax bared his teeth and sank his fangs into her shoulder over his mate mark. Sable screamed, arching up as she came, and he followed her over the edge, groaning loudly when he felt her teeth enter his shoulder.

"Mine," she whispered, licking over her bite after they were both spent.

"Always."

13

Sable kissed Dax gently on the cheek before slipping from the bed and getting dressed. Glancing back at her sleeping mate, she let a small smile tip the corners of her lips. After only a day, the man had stolen her heart. She knew mates fell in love quickly, with help from the mate bond, but this was just crazy. She'd never felt like this before, not even for Aiden, and she wasn't quite sure what to do about it. For now, she was going to just keep it to herself, she decided, sliding a knife into her boot, and her Glock into the holster at her thigh. Someday, she would tell him, but for now, it was too soon.

Leaving the room, Sable locked the door behind her, and met Silver out front by the car. "Let's get this done quickly," she said, looking back to the room her mate slept in. "He won't be happy if he wakes up and I'm gone."

Silver wagged her eyebrows, "Hell no, he won't be. What man wants to wake up alone after the time you just spent together?"

Sable felt a blush steal over her checks when she realized her friends must have heard everything she and Dax did through the thin walls, but she just shook her head and climbed into the car. She had several things to do in a very small amount of time. There was no way they were going to make it back to the coyote camp before nightfall if she didn't hurry, but she doubted Ebony would leave right away, anyway. And, if she did, then they would just have to track her.

An hour later, they were back with a rental car, clothes for Dax, Rubi, and Maya, and dinner. Entering the hotel room, Sable paused just inside, quickly scanning the area before shutting the door behind her.

"Where did you go?"

His voice reached her from the large bed, and desire curled in her stomach, sending tingling sensations straight to her clit. Pushing it down, she walked toward him, teasing, "I got you some clothes. I would prefer no one see what my man has to offer, except me."

When she got near the bed, he reached out and grabbed her, yanking her down beside him, and she couldn't help the giggles that slipped free. She couldn't remember the last time she giggled. She was a grown-ass woman. She laughed. Hell, sometimes she even snorted when her laughter got the best of her. She did not giggle.

"I prefer that, too," Dax growled, rubbing his scruffy face over her neck.

"Stop!" Sable cried, another fit of giggles overtaking her. "That tickles!"

Dax rolled over, pulling her on top of him, and she couldn't stop herself from running her hands down his chest. She was surprised to see some of the bruising already starting to fade. A small moan slipped free as she settled her jean clad crotch over his hard, thick cock, rocking slowly as she whispered, "As much as I want you, we need to leave soon or we won't be back to the coyote pack before dark."

Dax's eyes narrowed, and he nodded in understanding. Sliding his arms around her back, he pulled her down on top of him and held her close. "I can't ask you to go with me, Sable."

Nuzzling his cheek with her own, she murmured, "You didn't ask, Dax. I'm going, and don't try to stop me. You are my mate, and I'm not letting you go alone."

Sighing, he tightened his arms around her and rasped, "Thank you."

Rising up, Sable looked down at him in surprise. "You aren't going to fight me on it?"

Dax grinned, cocking an eyebrow, "Are you telling me I could win this argument?"

"Nope."

"Then why waste my time?" Shaking his head, he kissed her gently before letting go so she could get off the bed. "Besides, I want you with me. We just bonded, and I'm not ready to let you go."

"You better never be ready for that," she growled playfully, getting the bag of clothes she'd bought for him and tossing them on the bed. "I looked at the size on your old jeans, and guessed on your shirt size. Hopefully, they fit. There's also a toothbrush and some other things. I'll see you in the other room as soon as you are ready."

Leaving Dax to get ready, Sable went to check on the others. As soon as she entered the room, she knew there was an issue. The smell of fear permeated the room, and Maya was nowhere to be found.

"She's in the bathroom," Charlotte said quietly. "She refuses to go with us."

"Why?" Sable asked in confusion. "She doesn't have anything to be afraid of. Her brothers will be there."

"I think that is what has her scared, Sable," Silver murmured softly. "She doesn't know what to expect. She's been with the coyote pack for so long, and I don't think they treated each other very well, family or not."

The door opened, and Dax walked in, his brows furrowing as he looked around. "What's going on?"

"I need to talk to Maya," Sable said quietly. Ignoring his raised eyebrows, Sable crossed the room and knocked softly on the bathroom door before slowly turning the knob and opening it. "Can I come in, Maya?"

Maya sat on the floor, fully clothed in one of the outfits Sable bought her earlier. Her legs were pulled up, her arms wrapped tightly around them, and her forehead rested against her knees. Her long, brown hair flowed around her in waves, and Sable could see that her entire body trembled.

Shutting the door behind her, Sable sat down beside the young woman, her back up against the wall. Pulling her own legs up, she wrapped her arms around them to mimic Maya's pose. "What's wrong, sweet wolf?"

At first, she wasn't sure if Maya was going to respond, and then she heard, "What if they don't like me?"

"Aiden and Xavier?"

Maya nodded, still not raising her head, as she whispered, "What if they hurt me?"

Sable stiffened, her heart going out to the obviously abused woman next to her. "Maya, no one in the White River Wolves pack will ever hurt you, especially not your brothers. They will kill anyone who raises a hand to you."

That got her attention, and slowly she raised her head and looked over at Sable. "Why would they do that?" she asked, her brow wrinkled in confusion.

"Because they are your brothers, Maya. In our pack, family is the most important thing. There isn't anything they won't do for you."

"Then, why didn't they come for me?" Maya whispered, her eyes filling with tears. "Why did they leave me there all those years with people who hurt me?"

"Oh, sweet girl," Sable whispered, slipping an arm around Maya's shoulders and holding her close, "your brothers just found out about you recently. Our alpha has been looking for you ever since you were taken, and I joined in the search a few months ago, but we didn't have any leads. Chase never told them about you, because they were already in so much pain."

"Why? Did someone hurt them, too?"

Sable sighed when Maya laid her head on her shoulder, and rested her cheek on Maya's soft hair. "Not physically. I hate to be the one to tell you this story, but it is obviously something that you need to hear. Years ago, when your mother was pregnant with you, your father came up with a plan to overthrow our alpha, Chase's father."

She heard Maya gasp in shock, and then whisper, "Why would he do that?"

"Titen wanted power, Maya. The need for it consumed him. Unfortunately, he sold our pack out to another one to get it."

"What happened?"

"The other pack attacked ours, with help from your father. Titen hid your brothers, and told your mother to stay in the house until it was all over. She was nine months pregnant with you at the time. The other pack was supposed to leave your family alone, but they turned on Titen, killing Lila and taking you."

"My mother's name was Lila?"

"Yes," Sable said, rubbing her cheek on the top of the girl's head. "I was young then, but I remember her. She was so kind and compassionate. She treated all of us pups as if we were hers."

"What happened to Titen?"

"He went rogue after your mother's death and your abduction, and became very dangerous, even murdering innocent people. A decision had to be made."

"He was killed," Maya said quietly.

"Yes," Sable agreed softly. "Chase's father was alpha at the time, but both he and Chase's mother were killed in the fight. Chase became alpha, and once everything came to light, and Titen went rogue, he had no choice but to put him down."

"It needed to happen."

"What?"

"I've seen rogue animals, both wolf and coyote, and what they can do. Your alpha made the only decision that he could. There was no redeeming my father. He made his own choices, and a lot of lives were lost because of it. Chase's decision to put him down was the only one he could have made."

"How did you get to be so wise at such a young age?" Sable whispered.

Maya shrugged, leaning more into Sable. "I guess I've just seen a lot."

"And you've been through a lot." It wasn't a question. It was obvious that the young woman had suffered these past twenty years.

"Yes," Maya breathed.

Closing her eyes tightly, Sable said, "Well, I can promise you that you will be treated like a princess from now on, Maya. Your brothers definitely want you with them. Chase didn't tell them because he knew they already harbored so much guilt over what Titen did, and there was pain and humiliation along with that guilt. If Xavier and Aiden had known about you, they would have done everything in their power to find you."

"Which one is your best friend?"

Sable smiled, knowing she referred to the conversation they had earlier that day. "Aiden."

"He's a good man?"

"They are both good men, Maya."

"And they won't hit me?"

"No one will ever hit you again. I promise you that."

Maya nodded, and raised her head to look at her. "Okay."

"Okay?"

"Yeah," Maya whispered. "I trust you. If you tell me I'm safe, then I believe you."

Sable hugged her close, wiping away the moisture from her cheeks. "You are definitely safe, Maya. Charlotte and Silver are going to take you home now. You will get to meet Xavier, along with his mate, Janie, and their little girl, Laynie. And Aiden will be there, too. They will all be so happy to see you."

"What about you?" Maya asked softly. "I feel better when you're around. Safer."

"I will be there before you know it," Sable promised. Rising to her feet, she pulled Maya up and gave her a quick hug. "Dax and I have something to do first, but he and I will be coming home as soon as we can."

Opening the door, her gaze immediately locked on Dax, and her heart stuttered in her chest at the pride that shone in his eyes. Pride for her. A slow smile spread across his face, and she couldn't help but return it.

She couldn't believe she had found her mate. The man that held the other half of her soul. She was looking forward to spending the rest of her life with him, but right now, they had other things they needed to concentrate on. Like finding his sister.

14

Dax stared through his binoculars at the campsite below, watching as Jasper stood staring pensively at something off in the distance. It wasn't long before he saw why. After waiting two days for the General's men to arrive, they were finally here. "They are coming in from the north," he muttered through the coms he and Sable wore.

"I see them. I'm going to try to get a little closer." Sable's soft response had him tensing. He'd fallen hard for his mate since meeting her, and it went against everything he believed in to be placing her in danger the way he was. He tried to be open and understanding, knowing that she was an enforcer for her pack and this was what she did, but he was a dragon warrior. The need to protect was ingrained deep inside him.

"Be careful, Sable," Dax growled, his hands tightening on the binoculars when he caught a glimpse of her several yards from where she was just five minutes ago.

"I'm fine, hot pants," she whispered, and he could hear the laughter in her voice. "I'll show you how fine later."

His groin tightened at the thought of just how his mate would show him. "Fuck."

Soft laughter filled the coms, and then, "Hush, my sexy dragon. I need to concentrate."

As Dax watched, a large, black SUV pulled into the camp, followed by two more. Driving right past the coyote alpha, they stopped in front of the barn. The back doors of the first vehicle opened simultaneously, and two men got out, immediately heading for the building. The General's men flooded out of the other two SUVs, and they quickly surrounded the small village.

"There are several of them, Sable," he warned quietly, as Ebony appeared from the passenger side of the vehicle. The driver's door opened, and an intimidating looking male stepped out, slamming the door shut behind him. Dax's jaw clenched tightly as he took in the cold, calculating eyes of the man through his binoculars. They were hard, showing no mercy. He was strapped with several knives and at least three guns that Dax could see, and he had a sword in a scabbard on his back. There was no doubt in Dax's mind that he would be a force to be reckoned with.

"I see them," Sable murmured after a moment.

"The man that stayed with Ebony is the one we need to worry about," Dax growled, his eyes never leaving the male. Dark brown eyes surveyed the woods around them slowly, skipping over where Dax lay hidden, but he had a feeling his presence was known already by the soldier.

"His name's Jinx," came the soft response. "He's one of the General's top assassins."

"Shit."

"He's also on our side. Well, as much as he can be."

Dax stiffened when Jinx's gaze once again raked over the area, pausing about ten feet away from where he lay, and then moving on. "Explain," was his clipped response. The man before him was deadly. It was written all over his body. If they tangled, dragon or not, he would be in for one hell of a fight.

"He's Chase and Angel's son."

"Your alphas?" Dax asked in surprise.

Sable sighed softly through the coms. "Yeah. It's a long story, but what you need to know now, is that we can trust him."

"Trust one of the General's men?" Dax growled darkly. "I don't give a fuck whose son he is, Sable, he works for the man who is holding my sister hostage. Hell, he's probably had a hand in torturing her!"

"Dax, get a hold of yourself," Sable snapped. "Right now, Jinx is with the General because he has no choice. He's a good man."

"There is always a choice," Dax snarled, his chest heaving in anger.

"No," his mate whispered softly, "there isn't. Trust me, Dax. Please. Before you get us both killed. I promise to explain it all to you later."

Dax stiffened, the threat to his mate's life pulling him out of his red haze of rage. She was right. He was becoming reckless in his anger, which could draw attention to them at any time. "I'm sorry, baby," he muttered, taking a deep breath and letting his gaze settle back on the scene below. "I do trust you."

"Good," she breathed into his ear. "Time to be silent. I'm moving closer."

"I don't think that's a good idea."

She was already close enough. She was going to accidentally alert the enemy of her presence if she wasn't careful. When she didn't reply, he clenched his jaw tightly shut, unwilling to put her in any more danger than she already was.

SABLE CAREFULLY CREPT toward the camp as quietly as possible, until she was close enough to hear their voices. Her heart thundered in her chest, but she refused to turn back. She was going to help Dax find his sister, no matter what.

"We're here for the prisoners," Ebony stated, flipping her long hair over her shoulder as her gaze slowly raked around the area.

"We have a problem," Jasper told her, wiping his palms on his jeans nervously.

Ebony placed her hands on her hips and cocked an eyebrow. "What exactly is the problem?"

"They're kinda gone." Jasper's mate said, clinging tightly to his arm.

"What do you mean they are kind of gone?" Ebony asked coldly. "They either are, or they aren't."

"They're gone, boss," one of the General's men said as he exited the barn. "The place is empty. Just a lot of blood in the middle of the barn floor."

"Whose blood?" Ebony demanded, glaring at Jasper.

When he didn't respond right away, Ebony stepped closer to him, her hand going to a gun at her waist.

"A couple of my men," Jasper admitted, the stench of his fear filling the area.

Jinx cracked a smile, then threw his head back and laughed. "So, they got the jump on you, huh? Your men couldn't handle two people who were starved, beaten, and chained up?"

"They had help," Jasper's mate said, moving closer to him. "They had to have, because that other bitch is missing, too."

"What other bitch?" Ebony ground out, taking a step in her direction.

"A wolf that's been living with us since she was a pup. She's useless. Worthless. One of the old ladies here felt sorry for her and kept her around. She's nobody."

"Well, obviously she is somebody," Ebony interrupted. "If not, my prisoners would still be here, chained in that fucking barn where I left them."

The woman swallowed noticeably before replying, "She's just a scared, docile wolf."

"It wasn't just them," Jasper interjected. "There were other scents in the barn. More wolves."

"Did you trail them?'

"We tried. We tracked them through the woods to the road, but then we lost them."

Sable was having a hard time hearing, so digging her elbows into the dirt, she army crawled a little closer.

"That's enough," Dax hissed through the coms.

Stiffening at the direct order from her mate, Sable stopped, her eyes on the woman not far from her.

"Obviously, your mangy mutts don't know what the

fuck they are doing then," Ebony snarled, turning to Jinx. "Take a couple of the men and sweep the area! Find out where they went. Now!"

Jinx raised an eyebrow at her, then leaned back against the SUV, crossing his arms over his chest and spreading his legs out slightly in front of him. "I don't take orders from you, Ebony."

"Dammit, Jinx," Ebony snapped, stomping her foot in anger, "I am the General's daughter!"

"That means absolutely nothing to me," Jinx drawled, his gaze leaving her to canvas the area. A shiver ran up Sable's spine at the power that seemed to flow from him. Even though she knew he was on their side, he still scared her, almost as much as he pissed her off sometimes. There was no doubt in her mind that he not only knew that she and Dax were there, but also knew exactly where they both were. She also knew that he wouldn't give them away unless he had no choice. That, she was positive of. She hated that he worked for their biggest enemy, but she also understood why he did it. Without him on the inside, they would have lost a lot of their people already. If anyone could take that bastard down, it would be Jinx.

Suddenly, Ebony stiffened, and turned slowly to sweep the area with a dark, cold gaze. When she stopped, her eyes falling to where Sable lay hidden under a brush pile, Sable knew she'd been made. "Dax, I'm so sorry," she whispered softly. "I think I fucked up."

15

Dax cursed darkly, trading his binoculars for the Glock hooked to his side when Ebony's voice rang out, reaching him clearly. "If you want to live, you will surrender now." When Sable didn't move, Ebony raised her gun, waving it around in the air. "Let's try this one more time. Show yourself, and you may get the chance to walk away from this."

"Bullshit," Dax snarled lowly, his entire body taunt with tension. There was no way that bitch was going to let Sable go free if she found her. "I'm coming your way, Sable. Move back toward me, slowly."

"Dax, stand down. We may never be able to track down Raven if you show yourself."

"We will find out where they are keeping her another way."

"How? What if there is no other way? Maybe if I let them catch me, they will take me to wherever she is being held. Then you could follow."

"No way in hell," Dax snapped. "That is not an option, Sable!"

"But, Dax, your sister..."

"No." He would have to find his sister another way. There was no way he would allow Sable to be captured. Who knew what she would go through before he could get to her again? As much as he hated the thought of leaving his sister in hell for a while longer, he didn't see any other option. "I'll be there soon. Start backing up to me, Sable."

"It's too late, Dax. She knows exactly where I am."

"How the hell would she know that?" he demanded, trying to keep his voice low. "I can't even tell where you are, and I know the direction you were moving when you left me and put yourself in danger!"

"Let me show you what happens to people who don't listen to me, shall I?" Ebony drawled, before turning and pointing her gun toward Jasper.

"No!" his mate cried, clinging tightly to him. "He has done everything the General's asked of him! He can find you more men and women. He's valuable to you."

Ebony shrugged, the side of her mouth kicking up in a grin. "You're right." There was a loud crack as Ebony pulled the trigger. A bullet left the chamber of her gun, finding a home in the middle of the woman's forehead. "Jasper is valuable to the General, but you aren't."

"What the fuck!" Jasper yelled, catching his mate's lifeless body as she fell to the ground. "Darla! Darla!"

"Quit blubbering like an idiot," Ebony ordered, "or you will be next."

Jasper turned grief-stricken eyes in her direction, and slowly laid Darla onto the ground. Rising, he bared his fangs as he reached for his gun, and growled, "I will fucking kill you for this."

Shaking her head, Ebony raised her weapon and fired again. Jasper's eyes widened in surprise, and a moment later he was on the ground, next to his mate, his sightless gaze staring off into nothingness.

"That woman is a bitch," Dax muttered, crouching as low as he could, and slowly beginning to make his way to where Sable still hid. "I'm coming for you, baby," he promised. "Stay down, and don't respond to her."

"That isn't going to work if she starts firing over here," Sable said dryly.

"She can't know exactly where you are."

"She can if she has psychic abilities," Sable argued. "And if she is the General's daughter, she has to have some gifts. That's what he specializes in. Breeding future soldiers from people who have shifter genes and psychic gifts."

Dax frowned, moving quietly through the trees, careful to stay hidden the entire time. "Does that mean she is a shifter, too?" He didn't remember smelling an animal on her.

"No, I don't think so, which means she has to be psychic in some way."

"Come out, come out wherever you are," Ebony sang, moving closer to where Sable lay.

"You're fucking crazy, you know that right?" Jinx drawled, shaking his head.

Dax paused, his eyes narrowed on the man, waiting for him to make a move. When all he did was stare at Ebony, Dax slipped forward a few more steps.

"But, like you remind me on a daily basis, you are the General's daughter."

Ebony swung around, her revolver now pointed at Jinx. "Maybe I should put the next bullet in you instead."

Jinx raised an eyebrow, and slowly straightened away from the SUV. "Do you really want to go there, Ebony?"

"He's giving us a chance to get out of here," Sable whispered.

"Are you sure?" Dax paused, Glock in hand, as he waited for Jinx's next move.

"I'm not afraid of you," Ebony snapped, taking a step closer to Jinx, keeping her weapon trained on him.

"You should be," Jinx said, and then he moved so fast, Dax almost missed it when he swiftly removed the sword from his back and sliced the blade down, right into Ebony's gun, knocking it to the ground. As Ebony stared in shock, Jinx slid the sword back into the scabbard, and then closed the distance between them, until they were nose to nose. "If you ever pull a gun on me again, you better be prepared to use it."

Ebony shook with fury, and she raised a fist as if to strike Jinx.

"Do you really want to do that?" Jinx's tone was ice cold, and Dax froze when he saw the man's eyes flash from their normal brown to a bright green as he glared at Ebony.

"Please tell me you are close," Dax muttered into the coms, his gaze never leaving what was happening between Jinx and Ebony.

"I'm coming," Sable assured him, just as Ebony let out a string of curse words that would make a sailor proud.

Grabbing a gun at her back, Ebony swung around and pulled the trigger several times, aiming right where he was sure his mate had just been. At least, he hoped she wasn't still there.

"Sable," Dax snarled, grasping the Glock in his hand tightly, ready to rush everyone in the camp to save his woman.

"Shit, Dax." Her voice was filled with pain, and something he hadn't heard from her since they met. Fear. Rage filled him when she cried out in agony. Not giving a shit how many of the General's men saw him coming, Dax took off at a dead run through the trees, fighting to get to his mate.

"I got you, bitch!" Ebony screamed, firing again.

"Dax," Sable gasped, a low moan filling his ear. "Can't move. Hit too many times."

When she cried out again, Dax let out a roar that echoed throughout the forest. Giving in to the urge to shift and protect the woman who was his world now, he let his claws lengthen, and sliced through his shirt and then the side of his jeans.

"It's the man from the barn," someone called out, but Dax didn't slow down. Why the hell had he let her get so far away from him? He knew better, dammit!

"I'm coming for you, Sable," he ground out through large fangs that had dropped.

"Dax…"

"Holy fuck! What is he?"

"Who cares what he is?" Ebony yelled. "Shoot him!"

Dax let out another roar when he spotted his mate's hand lying limply on the ground, peeking out from under a large bush. Unable to hold his dragon back any longer, he dropped his gun and let the change take over. One minute he was standing there, his clothes barely hanging on him, and the next, a large, angry, fire breathing monster was in his place.

"Oh, my God!"

Dax paused, swinging his huge head around to look at Ebony. Satisfaction filled him when he saw her trembling in fear. Rising on his back legs to his full height, Dax threw his head back and trumpeted his anger to the heavens, and then closed the distance between them. Reaching out, he swatted her hard, sending her flying a few feet in the air. He watched as she slammed into the side of the SUV, and crumpled to the ground. Then, he went hunting.

The first person he got to suffered greatly when he wrapped his huge jaws around him and bit down, ignoring the shots that rang out, and the bullets that hit his thick scales. The second death was much quicker, with a thick claw slicing through a coyote's throat. The next had his heart removed. Then, he took to the air, and several more were consumed by his fire, as was the barn he and Rubi had been held in, along with several of the small huts, and anyone who was still in them.

There was a reason you never pissed off a dragon. By the time he was done, every coyote, along with all of the General's men, were dead. The only people left were Ebony and Jinx. Breathing heavily in anger, he closed the distance between himself and Ebony, stopping right in front of where the woman still lay passed out cold, before bellowing his rage.

"Wait, dragon! You need to stop! Killing Ebony will not help your mate. She needs you now."

Turning his massive head to look at the one they called Jinx, Dax bared his teeth. "I know, man. Trust me, I get it. I've wanted to take my sword to the bitch myself several times, but it won't help our cause if you do. There are things you don't know about her, dragon. I need her alive."

Dax cocked his head to the side, listening intently, even though all he wanted to do was rip out the woman's throat after what she did to his Sable.

"Let me worry about Ebony. Right now, your mate needs you. She isn't going to survive if you don't get her to the White River Wolves doctor quickly."

As Jinx spoke, he moved to the back of the SUV, opening it up and pulling out a small, black bag. Dax growled in warning when the man turned to go to Sable. Jinx glanced back over his shoulder, but didn't stop. "Look, I know you have no idea who I am, and no reason to trust me, but your mate does. She knows I would never intentionally hurt her, or anyone in her pack. They're my pack, too."

That stopped Dax in his tracks. He knew Jinx was Chase and Angel's son, but for some reason, he never associated him with being part of the White River Wolves pack. Probably because he worked for the devil. But, Sable loved her pack. She said they were her family. If he was family, then he would fight for her, wouldn't he? He would want her alive and safe. Shaking his head, Dax bared his teeth again when he saw that Jinx had reached Sable, and was kneeling down beside her.

"She's lost a lot of blood," Jinx called out, opening the bag and removing something from it. "There are five points of entry that I can tell, and only two exits. That means she still has three bullets in her. I'm afraid I will cause more problems if I try to remove them now. I am going to bind her wounds the best that I can and give her something for the pain. You need to get her to Doc Josie right away, or she might not make it."

Another loud roar split the air, this time one of pain and agony at the thought of his beautiful, spitfire of a mate not living another day. Dax needed to hold her. To tell her how much he loved her, and couldn't be without her. He needed to say so many things, but he couldn't in dragon form.

When he began to shimmer, initiating his shift, Jinx's voice interrupted him. "No, wait! You have to fly her there. It will be faster than driving, and there is no way you will get her on a plane like this."

Ignoring him, Dax let the change take him, and soon was standing buck ass naked in front of the guy. "Sable," he gasped, stumbling over to his mate and collapsing on the ground beside her. "Sweet Sable."

"Sweet?" A rough laugh left Jinx as he removed a syringe from the bag. "Not a word I would have ever associated with your woman."

Gently stroking a hand over Sable's thick, dark hair, Dax growled, "You obviously don't know her like I do." When Jinx slid the syringe into Sable's arm, Dax was unable to suppress the growl that erupted from his throat.

"It's just for pain," Jinx promised. "She's been shot five times, man. She has to be hurting." Glancing his way, Jinx raised an eyebrow. "Speaking of hurting, how are you doing, dragon?"

Dax spared his body a look, before shrugging, "I will be fine."

"You're covered in blood."

"You don't worry about me, wolf," Dax snarled. "Worry about my mate!"

Jinx nodded, throwing the syringe back in the bag, and pulling out some large bandages and a roll of gauze. "As long as you can make it to the White River Wolves compound."

"I'll make it."

"Dax."

Sable's voice was thin and rasping, but a miracle to Dax's ears. Leaning down, he pressed his forehead to hers and whispered, "I'm so sorry. I never should have let you get so far away from me."

"Not your fault," Sable whispered, a lone tear sliding down her cheek. "Hurts."

"I know, baby. Jinx gave you something for the pain."

"Jinx."

"I'm right here, Sable," Jinx said, as he began working on a wound on her arm.

Sable turned her head to look at Jinx, and Dax flinched at the raw pain in her eyes.

"Jinx, we need your help."

"I'm doing what I can, Sable. Your mate is going to have to shift again and fly you home. I can't do anything else here. You need surgery and blood."

"No," Sable gasped, another tear slipping free, as she struggled to sit up.

"You have to calm down, Sable," Dax ordered gruffly when blood began to seep through the white bindings.

Nodding, Sable swallowed hard, and turned to Jinx again. Her tongue snuck out to wet her lips, and then she rasped, "The General has Dax's sister, Jinx. You have to find her. Please, find her. For me."

Jinx looked at Dax in confusion, all the while quickly covering the rest of her wounds. "Your sister? The General doesn't have any dragon shifters. If he did, I would know."

"He has Raven," Sable insisted, a moan slipping out when Jinx began to bandage the last gunshot wound on her leg. "He does."

"Raven?"

"That's enough," Dax interjected, rising to his feet. "I have to get her to a doctor."

"Yes, and you need to leave now," Jinx agreed. "She's lost too much blood, Dax. You need to hurry."

"Jinx," Sable whispered, reaching for him. "Please, you have to find Raven."

Jinx captured her hand in his and squeezed it. "I will look for her," he promised, before standing and lifting her in his arms.

Another protective growl left Dax when Sable cried out in pain, and then went limp as she lost consciousness.

"We don't have time for a pissing match, Dax. Shift now, if you want your mate to live."

Fear filling him at the seriousness in Jinx's voice, Dax did as he was told, and was soon once again in his dragon form. He listened carefully to the directions Jinx gave him to the White River Wolves compound, and gathered Sable in his arms when Jinx handed her over.

"Dax." When he turned to look at him, Jinx took a step back before saying, "I will see what I can find out about your sister."

There was something in the man's eyes, something

that bothered Dax, but he didn't have time to figure it out. Knowing Sable's life had to come first, Dax bowed his head to Jinx, and then took to the skies, holding his mate close to keep her safe as he flew hell-bent toward her home.

16

Chase raked a hand through his hair in frustration as he stared across his desk at the young wolf in front of him. He had other, more pressing shit to deal with right now than the pup's incessant questions. He knew he was worried about his friend, but this was getting ridiculous. "Aiden, for the last time, Sable is on a mission. She will be back when it is completed."

"I haven't heard from her since she left, Alpha. That isn't like her."

"Well, I have," Chase told him, "and she is perfectly fine."

Aiden stiffened, and his eyes narrowed, "Then, why hasn't she called me? Or sent me a text?"

Sighing, Chase rose from his chair and crossed the room to stand in front of the window. He knew why Sable wasn't calling Aiden, but it wasn't his place to tell him. "Aiden..." Before he could continue, his phone began to ring. Hoping it was Angel, because it has been over a week since he'd last heard from her, he quickly retrieved his cell from his pocket and answered. "Chase here."

"Chase, it's Jinx."

"Jinx? What's wrong?" He could hear the urgency in his son's voice, and his hand tightened on the phone, nearly crushing it, when the response came through.

"Sable's been injured, Chase. It's bad. I did what I could for her, but she's lost a lot of blood. Her mate is flying her there now. He left a while ago, but this is the first chance I've had to call because I was dealing with Ebony. You need to tell the doctor to get her ER prepped and ready to go. He should be there soon."

"Flying?"

"Yeah. And Chase, you need to be careful. He is one protective, pissed off dragon."

"Shit."

"Dragons are very dangerous when they are angry. And this one is more than angry. He took out every single one of the General's men, along with a majority of the coyote shifters here, in a matter of minutes. You need to proceed with extreme caution when he arrives. The only thing on his mind will be protecting his mate, and it will be hard for him to differentiate between you wanting to help her, and you wanting to cause her more harm."

Chase froze when he heard a loud roar that nearly shook the walls of his building. Turning back to the window, he glanced up and his eyes widened in awe. Hovering above the compound was something he never thought he would ever see in his life. A large, beast, covered in red, gold, and orange scales, flew in circles, breathing long streams of fire as he bellowed his rage for all to hear.

"Fuck."

Chase looked back at Aiden, who now stood just behind him staring up at the sky, and nodded. "You got that right, pup. We might all be fucked."

He was finally at the White River Wolves compound, and he was exhausted. He'd flown fast and hard the entire way, his mate's life resting in his hands. She hadn't stirred since they left, and he was terrified. If she didn't make it, it would take more than the wolves below to take him out. The rage and fury that poured through him was like the hot fire he was releasing for the world to see. He knew he needed to stop, but he was beyond reason. The beast was in control.

Letting out another loud roar, Dax flew over the compound, his eyes on the buildings below. There was a large crowd gathering, watching him in both fear and excitement. He ignored it all. His mate was hurting, possibly dying, in his arms. Blood seeped through the bandages. Her life's blood, taking her from him. To a place he would follow if it came to that. He couldn't live without her. He wouldn't.

"Dax! Dax!"

Dax shook his head roughly, struggling to break free of the fogginess in his mind. He knew that voice. Had heard it before.

"Dax, you need to bring Sable down here, son! Bring her down here so we can help her."

Son? Another loud roar broke free at the word. His father was dead to him. He'd disowned him the moment he found out his parents sold his sister. He was no one's son. Racing toward the voice, he flew low and blew another stream of white hot fire out above the throng of people, heading for the male that was several yards in front of them, as if protecting them.

The man didn't move. He stood tall and brave, not even ducking when the fire came close. "Dax, I can't help Sable if you don't bring her to me. I am her alpha! I will keep her safe. You need to trust me!"

Trust him? Everyone wanted his fucking trust. And where had that gotten him? Raven was kidnapped, and living in hell. Rubi was injured. Who knew how bad? And his mate, his beautiful, courageous mate, was bleeding out in his arms.

Taking to the skies, Dax flew in a circle high above, before dropping down to hover over the man again. All the while, he kept his precious bundle snug against his chest.

"Dax, I promise you, I will keep her safe. She is one of mine. I will protect her."

Protect her? No one could protect her like he could. Dax tightened his hold on Sable. He hadn't done a very good job of keeping her safe against Ebony, though, had he? His woman was dying, and it was all his fault.

"Dammit, man! You need to give Sable to us so we can get her to Doc Josie!"

Dax's head swung around to meet the new threat that ran forward, stopping just behind his alpha. Brown hair, a lean muscular build, and brown eyes full of anger and concern.

"Don't antagonize him, Aiden!" Another voice yelled, and a man, almost identical to the first one, rushed forward, drawing a weapon as if to defend the other one. Aiden. He knew that name.

"Put your fucking gun away," the alpha ordered, waving a hand in their direction.

"He's going to hurt Sable if he doesn't stop breathing that damn fire all over the place," Aiden snapped.

"No, he won't," a small voice piped up. "His fire won't hurt her."

"Lily, stay back!" Chase ordered loudly.

"He's just confused, Uncle Chase. He won't hurt anyone. He's a good dragon. He protects the little princes and princess. He keeps them safe."

"What the hell is she talking about?" Aiden snarled.

The loud scream of a powerful engine broke through the conversation, and a black sports car roared through the compound gates, making its way toward them. It came to a screeching halt a couple of yards away, and the doors flew open.

"Daxton Dimitri Dreher, get your ass out of the sky, and bring your mate down here. If you don't, I'm coming up there after you! You know I will, brother!"

Dax heard the large gasp of the crowd, but his eyes were on the woman who stood below him, her long, blonde hair whipping out around her in the wind. Rubi was no longer the sister he had left behind when he went to serve his king years ago. She was now a dragon warrior, through and through. She was standing there, head held high, obviously in pain, but willing to challenge him for the sake of his mate if she had to.

"Dax, please, you have to bring her down," another voice called out.

He looked past Rubi to Maya, the sweet wolf they'd

rescued just days before from coyotes. How had she managed to turn out the way she did, after living with mongrels like that? The thought of the coyotes and their part in everything, infuriated him again, and he let out another loud bellow.

"I'm coming up there, Dax!" Rubi hollered, taking another step closer to him as she began to undo the buttons on her shirt. "I swear, I'm going to kick your ass, you idiot!"

Maya reached out and placed a hand on her arm, stopping her. Dax couldn't hear what she said to his sister, but when she came forward a moment later, stopping just a few feet from him, Rubi stayed back. "Dax, you need to listen to me. I know you are hurting. I know you are scared for your mate. But, you need to remember what she told us. This pack is her family. She loves them, and would do anything for them, as I'm sure they would for her."

"This is bullshit," Aiden broke in, taking a step closer to him. "Just give me Sable so that I can take her to Doc Josie."

"Aiden, shut the hell up!" his brother snarled.

Maya froze, her gaze leaving Dax and slowly going to the two brothers. But, then she seemed to catch herself, and she turned back to him. "Dax, you know who Aiden is. Think. He's Sable's best friend. He would never harm her."

Dax looked at the man who stood not far from him now, at the way he was willing to fight for Sable if he had to. Her best friend. The man she had thought she was in love with just weeks before. The man she would have chosen as a mate, if he hadn't come along.

"Dax, please. Give Sable to my brother. He will protect her until you are able to. She trusts him. You know you can, too."

Ignoring the look of shock that Aiden shot Maya's way, Dax slowly dropped to the ground, bowing his head in the man's direction. Maya was right. Aiden would take care of his mate for him until he was able to.

"Go get her, Aiden. Everyone else, stay back," Rubi ordered, slowly making her way around Maya, coming toward him. "His dragon knows you will protect Sable, but it is going to be hard for him to hand her over to you."

He watched Aiden closely as the man tore his gaze from Maya, and then quickly closed the distance between them.

"I promise, I will keep her safe," Aiden vowed, stopping just in front of him.

It took everything he had in him to hand his reason for living over to the man in front of him, but Dax did it. For her. When Aiden took Sable gently in his arms, Dax stretched out his long neck to gently rub his nose on her arm.

"Why don't you shift and come with us, big brother?" Rubi asked softly, moving in closer. Slowly, she reached out and placed a hand gently on his side, a frown appearing on her face. "Dax?" she whispered, pulling her hand back, covered in blood. "Dax!"

Dax rubbed against his mate one more time, before stepping back. Stumbling, he tried to catch himself, but it was too late. Collapsing to the ground, he finally acknowledged the agony that racked his body, and the exhaustion flowing through it. His mate was going to be safe. That was all that mattered.

"Dax! Stay with me! Dax! Please, don't leave me!"

A weak groan of pain left his throat, and then he fell to his side, his head lying on the soft grass. He fought to keep his eyes open as he watched Sable's friend rushing her down the hill, away from him, a woman at his side.

"Take it easy, big guy," Chase said, leaning down to place a hand gently on his neck. "You are a part of my pack now. Under my protection. Rest. Trust me to handle everything."

A huge shudder ran through his body as he felt the alpha push his calming power into him. It was like nothing he'd ever felt before. His last thought was of Sable, before his eyes closed and the darkness took him under.

17

Sable gazed at the man who sat in the chair next to her hospital bed, a soft smile on her lips. He had flown close to two thousand miles, severely injured himself, to bring her to Doc Josie. The good doctor had first saved her life, and then his. He was there when she woke up three days ago, and every single time since then. Even though she was feeling much better, he still refused to let her leave the hospital.

"How are you doing?"

Sable glanced over to see Aiden hovering just inside the door. It was the first time he'd come to see her since she'd gotten out of surgery. Gesturing for him to come in, she raised her bed into a sitting position and grinned. "I'm good. Wonderful."

Aiden grinned, his brown eyes dancing as he stopped beside her bed. "I'm glad." She could tell he meant it, but she could also tell that something was bothering him. There was a sadness deep within, that he was hiding behind his happy façade.

"Me, too," she whispered, reaching out to take his hand. "It's good to see you, Aiden."

"You, too." His voice was quiet, and she could see a muscle tick in his jaw.

"How's Maya?"

Sighing, Aiden shrugged. "I honestly don't know. She's hiding from us right now."

"Hiding?"

"Chase gave her an apartment near Xavier and Janie's, but she hasn't come out of it except to check on you and Dax." He hesitated before admitting, "I think she's afraid of us, Sable."

Sable nodded, squeezing his hand gently. "She's been through a lot, Aiden. Just give her time."

Aiden nodded, his eyes meeting hers. Hesitating, he asked, "Sable, are we good?"

Taking a deep breath, Sable glanced over at Dax before replying, "Aiden, I need to tell you something." While he waited patiently for her to collect her thoughts, she looked over at her mate again. He was everything to her now. All she had ever wanted in a man, and so much more. Her gaze going back to Aiden, she gently tugged her hand from his before saying, "Aiden, I left Colorado for two reasons. One, was to find your sister."

"That was the mission that Chase and Angel sent you on?"

"Yes. I'm sorry I had to keep that from you, but I didn't want to get your hopes up. I wasn't sure if we would actually find her, especially when we kept running into dead ends."

"I understand."

Swallowing hard, she admitted, "But, I was going to leave anyway, Aiden. This just gave me a good reason to."

"Why?" Aiden asked in confusion. "Why would you want to leave your family and friends? You love it here."

"I do," Sable agreed, her eyes once again drawn to her dragon. "Even after what happened to me years ago, I still couldn't leave."

"Xavier and I took care of those bastards, Sable," Aiden growled. "They will never hurt you again."

A low growl came from the chair next to her, the only indication that Dax was listening to them, even though she'd known the entire time that he was awake. The minute Aiden entered the room, his instincts to protect his mate had risen, and he'd woken.

"I know you did," she whispered, reaching for Dax. Past memories flooded in, coming back to haunt her, and she needed to feel his touch. "Dax."

His head came up, his eyes glowing a dark emerald color, and then he was out of the chair and sliding into bed next to her, pulling her close. Snuggling into him, she laid her head on his shoulder and wrapped an arm around his waist, careful not to touch any of the bandages on his body. "I'm right here, sweetheart," he said gruffly, kissing her gently on the top of the head.

"I'm sorry," Sable whispered to Aiden after a moment. "It's hard to think back to those days."

"I shouldn't have brought it up."

"You didn't," Sable said softly. "I did." Tightening her arm on Dax, she screwed up her courage before she continued, "There was another reason I left, Aiden." When he just looked at her curiously, she whispered, "I thought I was in love with you." Another low growl rumbled in

Dax's chest, but he didn't interrupt her. "It wasn't until I met Dax that I understood the love I feel for you is nothing like the love you feel for a mate."

Aiden froze, and he seemed to catch his breath, his eyes darkening to a deep brown. "Sable, I didn't know."

"I know you didn't," she said, idly rubbing her hand across Dax's chest, wanting to feel closer to him. "And, it's probably better that way."

"Fuck, the way I acted, Sable. The bar. The women. I'm sorry. If I'd known…no wonder you were so pissed at me."

Sable shrugged, her hand rising to stroke the hardness of Dax's jawline, and then sliding into the hair at the back of his neck. "It wouldn't have made a difference, Aiden. You weren't my mate. I know now that it never would have worked, even if you had felt the same way." Tilting her head back, she smiled up at the man she loved with all of her heart. "There is a difference between the love of a friend, and the love of a mate. I'm so glad I figured that out. And, I hope you find the kind of love I have someday, Aiden. I really do."

"Me, too," Aiden said quietly, before taking a step back. "Hey, I have some things I need to do. I'll catch you guys later."

Sable whispered goodbye, her eyes never leaving the dark green ones in front of her. She heard the door shut, and knew they would be left alone for a while. The nurses only came to check on her a couple of times a day now, and they'd already been there for the morning visit.

Her heart was thundering in her chest, and there was only one thing she wanted right now. It had been so long since she claimed her mate. She wanted him. Needed him.

Letting her fangs drop, Sable licked her lips as she growled, "Mine!"

Cupping the back of her head, Dax guided her mouth to his shoulder, right above her mate mark. "Always, my love."

Sable sank her teeth in deep, her hand going to his large cock that was straining against the scrubs he wore. She moaned as he thrust into her, wanting to feel his skin against hers. Sliding her hand underneath the waistband of the pants, she wrapped it around his thickness and began to stroke him quickly as she ground her aching clit against the side of his leg.

"Sable!"

She growled when she felt him come, coating her hand, and then cried out when his own hand slipped inside the hospital gown she wore, his fingers sliding deep inside her.

"Need you," she gasped, moving her hips against his fingers. "Please."

"Don't want to hurt you."

"You won't," she gasped, arching into him. "It's been almost a week, Dax. I'm already feeling better than I was."

"Baby..."

"Now, Dax!" she ordered, grinding into his fingers as she covered his mouth with hers.

Dax growled, nipping at her lips as he slid the scrubs down, and then her gown up. Gently, he moved her over on top of him, and then lowered her onto his still hard cock. A loud moan tore from her throat as he slowly filled her, and she grasped his shoulders tightly to steady herself. Her eyes on his, she began to ride him slowly, soft cries slipping free.

"Sable," he groaned, gripping her hips and pushing up into her. "You feel so damn good."

Sable held on tight, ignoring the slight twinge of pain coming from a wound in her side. She needed this. Needed him. She'd never felt anything as wonderful as having Dax deep inside her, moving, calling her name. It was everything. Small flames licked up his arms, and transferred to hers. There was no pain, just pure bliss, as they lit up her skin.

"So close," she breathed, her entire body trembling with need. She was so close. "Please, Dax!"

She didn't have to ask twice. He knew exactly what she wanted. Just the touch of his fangs to her shoulder had her on the brink of an orgasm, and when he bit down, she flew apart in his arms, screaming his name.

LATER, safe in Dax's arms, Sable whispered, "I grew up in the White River Wolves Pack. People come and go, but not me. I've lived here my entire life. I went to school with Aiden and Xavier. Aiden and I have been best friends ever since I can remember."

"It's good to have friends like that," Dax said, rubbing his chin on the top of her head.

"Yes, it is," she agreed. "I have three older brothers, who all moved away after they met their mates. My parents now live in California with one of my brothers, so they can be near their grandchildren. I stayed here."

"It's beautiful here."

Sable nodded against his chest, clutching tightly to his arm before going on. "I used to be an elementary school teacher. I loved the children, loved teaching. Until…" A sob caught in her throat, a tear slipping down her cheek.

"You don't have to say anymore, sweetheart."

"Yes, I do," Sable whispered, closing her eyes and taking a deep breath. "There was a boy in my classroom who was having some trouble. At the beginning of the year he was doing wonderful, but then things began to change. His grades were slipping, he would show up to class in dirty clothes, and he was losing weight. I tried to talk to the school, but he was the grandson of a prominent man in town, and they didn't want to rock the boat." Leaning up, she looked at him, "Seriously, a child was in trouble, Dax, and they didn't want to 'rock the boat'."

Dax ran a hand gently down her hair, pushing a stray lock behind her ear. "What happened?"

"He came to school a week later with visible bruises on him, holding an arm that was obviously broken. He said he fell off his bike. I could smell the lie, Dax, and I could smell his pain." Swallowing hard, she whispered, "I decided, screw the school and what they thought I should do. I took him to the hospital. It turned out that not only was his arm broken, but there were bruises, both old and new, all over his body. He also had a cracked rib, and a slight concussion." Wiping angrily at the tears that were now flowing freely down her cheeks, she rasped, "Come to find out, his mother had fallen in with a local gang. She was using drugs and drinking a lot. She had no idea what was going on with her own child. The bastards took turns beating on him when she took him with her to the gang's hangout."

"You did good, baby," Dax said gruffly, gently rubbing

her back. "Getting the police involved was the only option."

Sable nodded, thinking back to that time she would rather forget. "I thought so, too. And, I wouldn't change anything that happened after that, because Manny got the chance at a better life."

"You are a strong woman with a good heart."

Sable held on tightly to him as she whispered, "I just couldn't stand seeing him so broken, Dax. It was horrible, and no one in that school would step up and help. After the police got involved, I was told that I could clear out my desk. I wasn't allowed on the premises anymore."

"You have got to be kidding me."

"No," Sable whispered, shaking her head as she struggled to find words to tell him what happened next. "I lost my job, and then, two days later, the gang kidnapped me, and I lost even more." Dax's chest vibrated with a deep growl, his whole body beginning to shake in anger. "It was hell, Dax," Sable rasped, pushing closer to him, wanting to crawl inside him where he would keep her safe. "They had me for three days before Aiden and Xavier found me. They rescued me, and brought me home, to Doc Josie. Then, they went back and took out the entire gang."

"Baby, I'm so sorry."

"Chase saved me," she whispered, lost in thought. "I was going downhill fast, locked deep inside myself, terrified to come out and face the world. Even my parents and brothers couldn't help. But, Chase never gave up. He came to see me, sometimes three or four times a day. Sometimes we would talk, most of the time we sat in silence. He fought for me, because that's the kind of alpha he is. When I finally decided it was time to fight for myself, he took me under his wing. Trained me, taught me to defend myself. I became an enforcer, because I want to save others like he saved me. I want to give them purpose, a reason to live."

Dax tilted her head up, looking deep into her eyes. "Baby, you are the most amazing woman I have ever met." Kissing her gently, he said, "I love you, so much, Sable, and I am going to spend the rest of our lives showing you."

Sable stared up at the man who held her heart, and whispered, "You are my everything, Daxton Dreher. My love, my heart, my soul, my fire."

18

Jinx stood over the comatose body of the General, wanting nothing more than to plunge a dagger into his evil heart. The sick son of a bitch had ruined so many lives, his included. Sometimes, when he was at his weakest moments, he allowed himself to wonder what it would have been like to grow up with a family who loved him. Waking up to his sister's laughter each morning, hugs from his mother, teasing from a father who taught him more than how to survive living a life of one of the General's assassins.

The bastard had stolen all of it from him, just like he had from so many others. Even his own daughters, Ebony and Amber. He didn't deserve to live. He'd caused so much suffering and heartache. Too much. Jinx was allowing him to live, just until he could find out who was really in charge of the operation the General was running. Once that information came to light, the fucker was dead.

His hand tightening on the hilt of the dagger at his waist, one he hadn't even been aware he held, Jinx took a step closer to the bed. It would be so easy to end the son of a bitch's life right then. So easy. But, then he might never find out who gave the orders from high above. Jinx frowned, slowly moving his hand from the dagger. He'd also promised Sable he would try to find Raven, and he always kept his promises. He'd heard the name Raven before. From the General's lips. If he killed him now, he might never find the female dragon.

Suddenly, the General's eyelids began to flutter and Jinx stiffened, quickly fading back into the shadows. He watched as the General's hand moved, a small jerk on the pristine white sheets, and then jerk again. Closing his eyes, he did something he hated to do, and never did unless he felt like he had no other choice. Merging his mind with the General's, he stayed just long enough to find out what he needed to know. The General was waking up, breaking free of the coma he'd been in since Chase practically tore his throat out. But, more importantly, he remembered. Everything.

Suddenly, the door slammed open and a doctor rushed in, going straight to the man in the bed. When he was followed by two nurses, Jinx did what he did best. He slipped silently from the room, leaving no evidence behind that he'd ever been there. Once he reached the end of the corridor, he slipped out his phone and dialed a number he had memorized.

"Yeah?"

"It's me. He's awake."

Make sure and visit my website for information on all of my books, and to sign up for my Newsletter where you will receive all of the latest information on new releases, sales, and more!

Website: **http://www.dawnsullivanauthor.com/**

I would love to have you join my reader's group, Author Dawn Sullivan's RARE Rebels, so that we can hang out and chat, and where you will also get sneak peeks of cover reveals, read excerpts before anyone else, and more!

https://www.facebook.com/groups/AuthorDawnSullivansRARERebels/

Dawn Sullivan

ABOUT THE AUTHOR

Dawn Sullivan has a wonderful, supportive husband, and three beautiful children. She enjoys spending time with them, which normally involves some baseball, shooting hoops, taking walks, watching movies, and reading.

Her passion for reading began at a very young age and only grew over time. Whether she was bringing home a book from the library, or sneaking one of her mother's romance novels to read by the light in the hallway when she was supposed to be sleeping, Dawn always had a book. She reads several different genres and subgenres, but Paranormal Romance and Romantic Suspense are her favorites.

Dawn has always made up stories of her own, and finally decided to start sharing them with others. She hopes everyone enjoys reading them as much as she enjoys writing them.

- facebook.com/dawnsullivanauthor
- twitter.com/dawn_author
- instagram.com/dawn_sullivan_author

OTHER BOOKS BY DAWN SULLIVAN

RARE Series
Book 1 Nico's Heart
Book 2 Phoenix's Fate
Book 3 Trace's Temptation
Book 4 Saving Storm
Book 5 Angel's Destiny

White River Wolves Series
Book 1 Josie's Miracle
Book 2 Slade's Desire
Book 3 Janie's Salvation

Serenity Springs Series
Book 1 Tempting His Heart
Book 2 Healing Her Spirit
Book 3 Saving His Soul
Book 4 A Caldwell Wedding

Chosen By Destiny
Book 1 Blayke

Made in the USA
Coppell, TX
19 August 2024